Dear Customer:

We at Harlequin are extre[...]
introduce our new series,
Temptation, in a very spe[...]
valued subscribers. As a home subscriber we
want you to be among the first to find out what
Harlequin Temptation is all about. And what
better way than to give you this complimentary
book.

Romance publishing today is exciting,
expanding and innovative. We at Harlequin
have responded to readers' ever-changing
demands by creating this new sensuous series.
Between the covers of **Harlequin Temptation**
you will find thrilling, irresistible stories to
stimulate your imagination and warm your
heart. For while styles in romance may change,
the message will always remain the same:
love is of the essence . . . . ,

We know you will find our new series a welcome
addition to your existing subscription. This
extension of our current romance lines
continues our commitment to you: to satisfy all
your romance-reading needs with books of the
highest quality. Our sincerest wish is that
Harlequin Temptation will bring you many
hours of the most pleasurable reading!

Kay Meierbachtol

Kay Meierbachtol
Managing Editor
Harlequin Temptation

THE AUTHOR

Maris Soule was born in Oakland, California, but lived in Santa Barbara for three important years—it was in graduate school there that she met her husband and was married. The Soules and their two children live in Michigan now, but Maris still loves the Santa Barbara area. She misses the walks along the beach and trips to nearby points of interest as well as the wharf area.

Maris confesses that she's always loved cats. When she was single and dating, it seemed as though her pets were always doing the wrong things—like Sam in *First Impressions*.

First Impressions

MARIS SOULE

HarlequinBooks

TORONTO • NEW YORK • LONDON
AMSTERDAM • PARIS • SYDNEY • HAMBURG
STOCKHOLM • ATHENS • TOKYO • MILAN

To Bill

Published December 1983

ISBN 0-373-25100-9

Printed in Canada

1

Tracy Dexter looked up from the table, her blue eyes sparkling like sapphires as she glanced around the faculty room. How quickly the summer had passed. It seemed like only yesterday she'd been saying goodbye to the other teachers and wishing their principal, Edward Holmes, a good retirement. Silently she'd blessed the old man for deciding to quit.

"Have you seen the new principal?" Rose Springer asked, pulling out a chair next to Tracy's.

"Not yet. Have you?" Tracy moved over to make room for the tall attractive redhead.

"No, his door was closed when I walked by."

All summer Tracy had wondered what their new principal would be like. Not as out of touch with teenagers as Holmes had been, she hoped. His lack of leadership had continually frustrated her. "Think the school board would hire another man as inept as Holmes?"

"I sure hope not," moaned Rose. "This Mark Prescott's got to be better. I just wish I could figure out why his name sounds so familiar." She took a cookie from the dish in the center of the table.

"No one seems to know him." Tracy eyed the brownie that was left on the plate, then remembered her diet. Although her slim shape looked perfect in her white cotton peasant blouse and blue-and-white dirndl skirt, she was determined to lose two more pounds.

"I was talking to Bob and he said Prescott's from Los Angeles." Rose brushed a few crumbs from her white harem jump suit, then sipped her iced tea.

At the mention of Bob Martin's name, Tracy glanced around the room for the counselor's familiar, rumpled blond hair. She smiled when she saw him, deep in conversation with the school's other counselor, Sylvia Johnson. As usual, Bob had his coat off and wore no tie.

In a hushed voice Rose asked, "How are Bob and his wife doing?"

Tracy's attention swung back to her friend. "Fine. That baby girl they adopted was just what Joanne needed."

"Now all we need to do is find a solution for *your* problems."

"I have no problems," Tracy assured her. "When I left Gerry, I became a new woman. No more being treated like a child; no more being suspected every time I look at another man."

"You certainly seem happier. How was your first summer as a divorcée?"

"Great." She couldn't help grinning, her tanned cheeks dimpling as she remembered shopping sprees in Santa Barbara, long walks along the beach and that wonderful sense of freedom. "I drove down to San Diego and spent almost a month basking in the sun, visiting mom. Would you believe it, she has another boyfriend."

"Someone she's serious about?"

"Oh no, I hope not," laughed Tracy. "I don't think I could take a fourth stepfather."

"So, what about you? Have you met anyone exciting?"

Tracy shook her head, her short, bouncy blond hair framing her face. "Rose, I'm not ready to get involved with another man." Knowing her friend was dying to hear something positive, she added, "My summer wasn't entirely dull. I did get propositioned."

A hush fell over the room, making her final words audible to everyone. Tracy blushed as she glanced at the other teachers. She'd never meant for them to overhear her statement. Then, for the first time, she saw the reason for the silence.

Filling the doorway was one of the most impressive men Tracy had ever encountered. His thick brown hair, so dark it was nearly black, was fashionably cut and styled, his skin tanned to a golden bronze. His tailored, gray tweed sports jacket covered a broad chest, and his gray slacks, cut in the European style, seemed to be molding his trim hips.

His eyes were what transmitted his power. Dark and piercing, they were directed at her, singling her out from the other teachers. Tracy's stomach tightened. It seemed an eternity that he gazed at her, then he looked around the faculty room, smiled and said, "Good afternoon. I'm Mark Prescott, your new principal."

As her own mouth dropped open in shock, Tracy heard the soft "wow" that escaped Rose's lips. Tracy had to agree. She certainly hadn't expected anyone like this. Mark Prescott appeared to be in his early thirties, and he looked more like a jet-set playboy than a principal.

Her heart was racing as she turned in her seat to watch him stride across the floor. Nervously she reached for her glass of iced tea, her mouth dry. Not once did her eyes leave his tall, lean form.

How she could have been so clumsy, she didn't know. It happened so quickly, there was no time to think. Her hand hit the glass; it teetered, then fell, spilling ice cubes and tea onto the table. With a gasp she pushed back her chair and jumped to her feet, trying to escape the brown river running rapidly toward the table's edge and her skirt.

Mark Prescott turned, a frown drawing his thick dark brows closer as he noticed the mess on the table—then who had caused it. "I'm sorry," mumbled Tracy.

"I'll get some towels," offered Rose, pushing her chair back and rising gracefully.

Immobilized, Tracy watched Mark as his gaze left her and followed Rose's progress. Boldly he let his eyes stray over her figure, slowly taking in each well-placed curve, and for an instant Tracy was jealous of her friend's beauty. Then she hurried to right her glass and gather up the ice cubes.

Quickly she and Rose mopped up the mess, threw away the sodden paper towels and returned to their seats.

"If you're ready," said Mark, glancing Tracy's way, "I'd like to start this faculty meeting. It's a hot day and I'm sure everybody would much rather be down at the beach than in here listening to me."

For the next few minutes he reviewed his own teaching background, his two years' experience as vice-principal at a high school in Los Angeles and his reasons for taking this job in Santa Barbara. His voice was deep and firm, his words concise and well chosen. Considering the positive way he'd taken command, it was evident that Mark Prescott was accustomed to giving orders. That would be different from Holmes.

Soon he was outlining changes he would be making in school policy. He strolled about the room as he talked, and with his lithe movements he reminded Tracy of a well-trained athlete. She'd been surprised when he said that he'd taught science. Mark Prescott did not resemble any of the stodgy old men who had taught her own high-school science classes. If anything, he looked more like a movie star, or at least a football coach.

As he discussed procedures for the first day of school, answering questions put to him by the staff, he called each teacher by his or her name. Obviously he'd done his homework and knew them better than they did him. Fascinated, Tracy couldn't keep her eyes off him.

In a way he reminded her of Gerry. Not that this man, with his dark, classic good looks actually resembled her ex-husband. But he had the same aura of assurance that had first attracted her to Professor Gerald White. Curiously she wondered if Mark's self-confidence was a facade, if underneath he was as neurotic and insecure as Gerry.

She'd learned a lot those four years she was married. She'd learned that just because a man was twenty years her senior didn't mean he was mature. Gerry had treated her like an adolescent, yet he was the one who hadn't grown up. He'd cried like a baby the day she told him she was leaving, that she'd had enough of his temper and jealousy. Never again would she idolize a man, as she had when she first met Gerry. Her learned professor of psychology had feet of clay, and so, probably, did Mark Prescott.

Tracy was frowning when Mark stopped in front of her. "You look uncertain," he said. "Is there something about my request you don't like?"

"I..." she stammered, not having the slightest idea what it was he'd requested. "I'm sorry, my mind wandered for a minute."

"I said that from now on I expect all teachers to remain in their classrooms for ten minutes after school's out," he repeated for her benefit. "That way any student who wishes to will be able to see you. In other words, no racing down to the faculty room for a smoke as soon as the bell rings."

"I don't smoke," Tracy replied defensively, feeling nervous under his penetrating gaze. "And I'm always in my room at least ten minutes after school's out. Usually longer."

"I'll vouch for that," injected Bob Martin.

Mark's attention left her as he looked across the table at the counselor. Bob grinned an apology for intruding into the conversation, his blue eyes twinkling. "You'll find Tracy's always available for the students—before and after school. She's a very conscientious teacher."

"Thank you for explaining the situation." Mark studied Bob for a moment longer, then nodded and glanced back down at Tracy. "I didn't mean to single you out. Those who are guilty know it and the rest of you, I hope, will continue the good job you're already doing."

Quickly he went on to cover additional changes he

expected initiated. Edward Holmes had avoided the classrooms, had rarely administered any discipline and had feared controversy. It was evident Mark Prescott was going to take a more active role in running Dos Pueblos.

For the most part Tracy wasn't bothered by the new edicts. She hadn't been one of the many teachers who had been sliding by under Holmes's indolence. She loved teaching and working with teenagers. Rather than seeing extracurricular activities as a bother, she'd always viewed them as an opportunity to get to know her students better. It was only when Prescott stated that he'd heard some teachers had bypassed the principal's office with their ideas that Tracy felt guilty.

All last spring, knowing Holmes would be retiring, she and Bob had planned and structured a class that Holmes would have rejected. Only by keeping the name vague and submitting a nebulous outline had they managed to get the principal to approve the class and schedule it for this year. Maybe Prescott had discovered their subterfuge.

The thought bothered Tracy, but she forced herself to set her worries aside and follow what was being said. She'd embarrassed herself enough for one afternoon.

The rest of the meeting went by quickly. In all it took less than an hour, a feat Holmes had never accomplished during Tracy's two years at the school.

"Don't forget my back-to-school party, two weeks from Saturday," announced Rose, standing up before the faculty began to leave. "Spouses and dates are also invited."

Walking over to Mark, Rose reached out and casually

touched the sleeve of his sports coat. "Mr. Prescott, I must say you're going to be a pleasant change from our last principal. Has anyone ever told you you look exactly like a darker verson of Robert Redford?"

Shocked by her friend's boldness, Tracy watched Mark's reaction. There were no signs of embarrassment. He smiled, his white teeth even and bright, and once again his eyes casually assessed Rose's perfectly made-up face and womanly attributes. His was not a lewd glance, Tracy noted; rather an appreciative analysis of a beautiful woman.

"Call me Mark. And thanks for the compliment. Robert Redford has always been one of my favorite actors."

"Every year after school's started I have a get-together for the staff. You and your wife are certainly welcome," invited Rose.

"I'm not married." He looked down at the graceful hand resting on his sleeve.

"Well, then," Rose returned, her voice low and silky as her long mascara-darkened lashes fluttered seductively over her milky white skin. "I hope you'll come so we can get to know *you* better."

"I'll plan on it," he said with a smile. "I'm looking forward to getting to know all of you."

"Mr. Prescott?" Jeff Black, the biology teacher, came to Mark's side, and Rose casually withdrew her hand and stepped back.

"Hey, Tracy," Bob Martin called, hurrying around the table. "Got a minute? I tried calling you several times yesterday, but you were never home." Reaching her side, he slipped his arm around her shoulders and gave her a squeeze.

Tracy saw Mark glance away from Rose and Jeff toward Bob and her. His brows drew closer, a slight frown crossing his face, then his attention returned to Jeff.

"I've missed you," Bob was saying, and the tone of his voice told Tracy he was worried about something.

"What's the problem?" she asked.

"Mind if we discuss it in my office?"

Together they started toward the counseling offices just outside the faculty room. As they passed Mark, Tracy glanced his way and caught him once again watching her, his firm lips drawn in a tight line. She wondered if there was a hint of disapproval in his dark brown eyes. And if so, why. The man didn't know her, couldn't possibly be in a position to judge her. She smiled politely and he nodded back, but there was no warmth in his expression.

In the office Tracy leaned against the desk as Bob closed his door, then came to her side. "It's Joanne," he began with a sigh. "I thought everything was going to be better now that we have Amy, but lately Joanne's been acting strange. She's always tired. In the last two weeks all she wants to do is sleep. Do you think it's psychosomatic? Has she reverted to feeling guilty because she couldn't have a child?"

"Don't go jumping to conclusions," warned Tracy. "Joanne's exhaustion could be due to any number of reasons. Maybe she's low on iron. Has she had a physical lately?"

"Not since we went through the adoption. I suggested she see the doctor, but she keeps putting it off. Listen, could you stop by and talk to her? Things have been going so well for us lately that I hate to have something go wrong now."

"How's Joanne feel about Amy?"

Bob sighed. "As far as I can tell, she adores the baby. We both do. And Joanne takes excellent care of her. She just doesn't have any energy left for anything else."

A glance at her watch showed it was nearly four. "I can't stop by today. I have a dinner date and lots to do before then. How about tomorrow, after I finish putting away supplies and getting my bulletin boards ready? I've been wanting to see Amy, anyway. I bet she's grown."

"Like a weed. Thanks, Tracy." Bob gave her hand a squeeze. "I don't know what I would do without you." Opening the door for her, he asked, "Anyone special tonight?"

Tracy shook her head. "Just George, from church. He knows I don't want to get serious, but he keeps asking me out. I think he's lonely."

"See you tomorrow," called Bob as she walked down the short hallway and past the main office.

The building was hot and stuffy. There was always a heat wave when school reopened, Tracy thought. She noticed their new principal was talking to Mrs. Baines, the school secretary. He'd removed his jacket and his shirt was sticking to his back, delineating broad muscular shoulders. His shirt sleeves were rolled up to his elbows, exposing tanned sinewy forearms covered with springy dark hairs.

Strangely, Tracy felt her pulse quicken as she studied his handsome physique. What was wrong with her? Hadn't she learned anything from her marriage to

Gerry? Good looks weren't enough. Tracy was sure she didn't want to get involved with Mark Prescott. She didn't want to get involved with any man. Her new-found freedom was too precious.

As if sensing her presence, Mark looked up, and when he frowned, Tracy knew she didn't have to worry. There was something about her he didn't like—some reason he disapproved of her. Perhaps she'd insulted him by not paying closer attention during the meeting. Or maybe it was the incident with the iced tea that had upset him. It could be, that, like Gerry, he saw her behavior as adolescent. If so, all the more reason to avoid him. Ignoring his dark countenance, she smiled and called out a friendly goodbye.

Outside in the parking lot Tracy paused, took a deep cleansing breath of salty sea air and pulled out a pair of dark glasses to protect her eyes against the brilliance of the sun. She hadn't been truly interested in a man for a long time, and her physical reaction to Mark Prescott disturbed her. She'd dated since her divorce—gone to dinners and shows, concerts and plays—but none of her escorts had stirred any emotional desires. That's why her response to this new principal surprised her. It was something she would have to analyze.

With long graceful strides she headed for her car. What she wasn't aware of were the dark brown eyes that followed her progress.

2

THE NEXT MORNING, as Tracy entered the main office of the one-story Spanish-style school building, Mark called from his desk, "Miss Dexter, may I see you?"

She exchanged a greeting with the gray-haired Mrs. Baines, who was busy sorting mail, then entered the principal's office.

"Close the door," ordered Mark, leaning back in his swivel chair and watching her with those dark penetrating eyes. "And sit down."

Obeying, Tracy pushed the door shut, then walked toward his massive oak desk, settling herself in a straight-backed wooden chair. Casually she crossed her legs.

Today was a workday, in preparation for Monday and the opening of school. Her choice of clothes had been dictated by comfort rather than fashion, and she was wearing her favorite pair of blue jeans and a pink cotton camisole. She'd washed and blow dried her hair before leaving her beach house, but her makeup was minimal. Tracy was certain the image she projected was both youthful and plain.

Not that she cared, she told herself. She wasn't interested in Mark Prescott and didn't want him interested in her. Still, as she glanced down at her sandals and noticed a chip in her toenail polish, she wished she looked a little more sophisticated.

"I'm sorry about yesterday afternoon," she told Mark. "About spilling the tea and not hearing what you said . . . I didn't mean to be rude."

"I never thought you did." He casually passed over her apology. "Actually, I've been looking through your file." His eyes were on an open folder on his desk. "Is this information correct? You received your teaching credential two years ago June from the University of California, here at Santa Barbara, and were hired to teach psychology and sociology?"

"That's right."

He scanned the material in front of him. "According to this copy of your application, your name is Tracy White."

"Yes," Tracy answered. "I was married when I started teaching. My divorce was final last fall. Dexter is my maiden name."

Mark looked up, his eyebrows rising as he appraised her. "You hardly look old enough to be a teacher, much less a divorcée."

"I'm twenty-five," she said defensively. *A failure, just like my mother.* Not that she would tell him that.

He leaned back, his elbows resting on the arms of his chair, his chin on the back of his folded hands. Silently he studied her until she fidgeted, recrossing her legs. Why had he called her into his office?

"My problem," Mark began, as if reading her mind, "is your sixth-hour class."

Tracy tensed. That was the class Bob and she had manipulated into the schedule. It was the class she wanted desperately to teach. "My Life class?" she asked hesitantly.

"That's the one."

He leaned forward, his pale blue cotton shirt stretching across his broad shoulders as he reached into a drawer and removed a folder. His sports coat was hung on a hook beside the closed door and he wore no tie, the top buttons of his shirt open, exposing a mat of dark hairs on his tanned chest. Tracy found it impossible not to stare at him, and color rushed to her cheeks when he looked up and caught her doing so.

There was a knowing half-smile on his lips as he sat back. She knew he'd seen her embarrassed reaction, but to her relief he said nothing. Trying to appear nonchalant, she focused her eyes on the sheet of paper he was pulling out of the folder. It was the list of speakers she'd requested permission to schedule for her sixth-hour class.

"I met with Mr. Holmes last week," Mark began. "We went over the classes scheduled for this fall." All traces of amusement had vanished from his features. "Holmes was quite surprised when he saw the speakers you've lined up for your Life class. It seems he was never completely informed about what you would actually be teaching."

He paused, and Tracy drew in her breath. From the sternness of his expression, it was obvious Mark was aware of the deception and disapproved. She said nothing.

"In fact," he went on, "Holmes became quite upset. He said you purposely gave him ambiguous information about the class, that you knew he opposed the teaching of sex. He said you and Bob Martin tricked him into approving the class."

"It's not a sex-education class," Tracy argued. "It's a general-information class about life—from birth to death. We'll talk about sex, but that won't be the only material we cover. I have units planned on family relations, teenage problems, drug abuse, self-esteem . . . ." She groped for words.

"Our students need help understanding themselves and the people around them. Holmes refused to approve any class material that might be slightly controversial. He was afraid of rocking the boat. When I heard he was retiring, I hoped the person taking his place would recognize the needs of these students—but I had to do something last spring if I wanted to teach the class this year. So, with Bob's help, I made the class outline look innocuous."

"In other words, you tricked Holmes."

Tracy sighed. The man seated across the desk certainly didn't appear to be the ray of hope she'd prayed would replace Holmes. His dark eyes were piercing hers, the straight line of his mouth showing no mercy. Instinctively she knew excuses would be futile, reasons superfluous. He'd asked if she'd tricked Holmes. There was only one answer.

"Yes," she said softly, dropping her gaze to the floor. Somehow she expected to hear a fist pound the desk, as her ex-husband had so often done when he was angry with her.

"At least you're honest about that," Mark said, a note of surprise in his voice. Tracy looked up quickly. He'd once again leaned back in his chair and was studying her.

"Holmes told me to cancel the class," Mark continued. "He said parents would object. What do you think?"

His change of attitude caught her off guard and she wasn't certain how to respond. "I think the class is necessary and shouldn't be canceled. There may be objections to some of the material, but I'd planned on sending a letter to the parents, informing them about what I would be teaching, how and why. If there was material they didn't want their child exposed to, they could call me and I'd arrange out-of-class alternative lessons for that unit."

"Sounds good," he nodded. "Mail the letters. Don't send them with the students."

"Then you're not going to cancel the class?"

A slight smile curved Mark's lips, but Tracy suspected he was amused by her surprise instead of being pleased by the situation. There was no warmth in his eyes.

"I want a complete outline of every topic you plan on covering in that class, what resources you'll be using and what you hope to accomplish." He paused, so his next words had more impact. "I mean an honest summary, not something you think will pass my inspection. Whether you like my way of doing things or not, I am now the principal and I won't tolerate subterfuge."

"I understand," Tracy responded, knowing she'd been reprimanded.

What could she say? After seeing how she'd tricked Holmes, he had every reason to mistrust her. She'd certainly made a poor first impression. "Is that all?" she asked, rising to her feet.

"No, that isn't all."

His tone was authoritative and Tracy sat down again. She watched him clasp his hands together as he looked at her, a frown once again furrowing his brow. At last he spoke. "Technically, what you do on your own time is none of my business. However, I hope you realize that when it affects this school it becomes my business."

His expression was disapproving. There was something else she'd done he didn't like. But what, Tracy wondered.

He answered her question before she had a chance to voice it. "Besides the business about your Life class, Mr. Holmes brought your relationship with Bob Martin to my attention."

"What relationship?"

"Come on, Tracy, don't be coy," demanded Mark, leaning forward and resting his elbows on his desk. "It's not uncommon for two teachers to have an affair, but not so blatantly when one is already married. Either you're being very naive or very foolish."

Tracy sat speechless for a moment, then struggled for a reply. "You're suggesting Bob and I . . . ."

"Are lovers," he supplied, then shook his head. "Frankly, the information surprised me. You have one of those sweet innocent faces, and if Holmes hadn't told me, I would have sworn you'd be the last person on this staff to be having an affair with a married man. However. . . ." He let the word hang like a judgment about to be pronounced.

"You can't be serious." Tracy wanted to laugh, but what he was saying was too vicious—too ludicrous to be funny. From the expression on his face, however, she knew he was very serious.

She stood, pushing back her chair. Anger darkened the blue of her eyes as she stared down at him. "Mr. Prescott, I don't care what Holmes told you. What you're accusing me of is ridiculous!"

"Is it?" He also stood—slowly and deliberately. Although Tracy was five foot seven, Mark towered over her. It was a psychological illusion of power, she was sure; one that he was consciously employing.

"Yes, it is!"

"Yesterday, after the faculty meeting, Bob and you couldn't wait to get into his office. I've been told you spend a great deal of time in there...with the door closed."

Cheeks flushed, Tracy looked up into his eyes, her chin raised in defiance. "Bob and I are friends. Men and women can be friends without being lovers. The time I've spent in his office involved a personal matter. The door was closed for privacy, not for sex."

His glance ran quickly over her, catching the toss of her hair as her head snapped back, the sparks of anger in her eyes and the straightening of her spine. "Then you deny you and Bob are having an affair?" He moved from behind his desk to stand beside her.

"Yes, I deny it." Boldly Tracy faced him. The top of her head barely reached his chin.

"You're telling me that Holmes made all this up? That Bob and you haven't been meeting regularly in his office, that you two don't eat lunch together and go off together after school?"

"No!—I mean yes," Tracy stammered, trying to find the right words.

She'd thought she was past the stage of getting flustered when falsely accused. Gerry had put her through this time and time again. At least Gerry, as her husband, had had a right. This man was hardly more than a stranger—even if he was her principal.

"Bob and I have spent a lot of time together, but not because we're lovers."

It would be easy to explain about Bob's marital problems, but Tracy considered those discussions a confidence—one she wasn't about to break. Turning away from Mark, she walked toward the door.

He stopped her before she turned the knob, his large hand covering her small delicate fingers. "I wasn't finished," he said calmly, his body blocking her exit.

"I was," fumed Tracy. "I've told you, Bob and I are not having an affair. I'm not going to spend all morning defending my innocence."

"Innocent or not, how it looks to the rest of the faculty and to the students can be just as damaging as if it were true. I've just arrived, yet I've heard about you two. I can imagine the gossip that must be going around the school."

Tracy closed her eyes. She'd never thought anyone would misconstrue her friendship with Bob. Sure, Rose had asked if something was going on between them, but that was Rose's nature. To Rose there was no such thing as friendship between men and women—only love and sex.

Standing in front of Mark as she was, his hand still covering hers, Tracy slowly became aware that neither

of them had said anything for some time. Opening her
eyes, she looked first at the small white buttons of his
shirt, then at the silky dark hair at his neckline. Finally
she gazed up at his face and felt her stomach muscles
tighten. He was such a handsome man. She was always
drawn to the virile type. The scent of his after-shave
reached her nostrils and a tingle of excitement ran down
her spine. Quickly she pulled her hand out from under
his.

"I hadn't realized anyone was talking about us,"
she managed, hoping Mark didn't sense how he was af-
fecting her physically. "I didn't know about any gossip."

"Now you do." His voice was softer as he watched
her. "You're a professional, Tracy. You say there's
nothing between Bob and you. I don't know if that's
true or not; however, I do expect you to conduct yourself so that there's no further cause for gossip." He offered a half-smile. "Now, as far as I'm concerned, the
subject is closed. If you need any help with that letter to
the parents, let me know. I'd like to read it before you
send it out."

"Because you don't trust me?" Tracy felt defensive.

"Because I like to know exactly what's going on, especially when it pertains to the school I'm in charge of. I
gather Holmes let a lot slip past. Be assured, that won't
be the case with me."

"I'll have the letter on your desk Monday morning. Is
there anything else, Mr. Prescott?"

Eyebrows raised, he studied her. "I don't want to start
the year as enemies, Tracy. Can't you call me Mark?"

"I find it difficult to be friends with a man who refuses

to believe I'm telling the truth." She'd tried that once. It had ended in a divorce.

"Then convince me. Have dinner with me tonight."

For a moment Tracy simply stared at him. Considering his attitude earlier, an invitation to dinner was the last thing she'd expected—or wanted. "I'm afraid not."

"Any particular reason why?"

She could think of several reasons not to date him, all very personal and none she wanted to discuss. "I have other plans," was her response.

"Then tomorrow night," he pressed.

"Mr. Prescott," her tone was exasperated, "I have no intention of going out with you tonight, tomorrow or any night. Long ago I learned not to mix business with pleasure. You are the school principal; I'm one of the teachers. Let's keep it that way."

"Think of all you may be missing, Miss Dexter."

A sensuous smile curved his lips, and Tracy realized at once that she had to stay away from this man. He could turn on the charm too easily. "Perhaps you're right, Mr. Prescott, but that's my decision. Is that all?"

"That's all." Mark opened the door and Tracy hurried past him.

She wanted to get out of his office—away from temptation. It would be a lie to say she didn't find him attractive or that she wasn't flattered by his invitation; yet she knew it would be disastrous to accept. Already he'd shown how similar he was to Gerry.

In the hallway between the main office and the faculty room Tracy paused. Mark had accused her of having an affair with Bob. Maybe people were gossiping about them. Maybe she had been naively closing her ears to what was being said.

It had been so good to have someone to talk to when she first came to Dos Pueblos—an understanding ear. Bob had been an empathetic listener. When they first met, Bob's wife, Joanne, had been in many ways the same as Gerry—jealous and insecure.

Funny, neither Joanne nor Gerry had had reason to distrust either one of them. Bob was a faithful and loving husband. He'd never think of having an affair—any more than she'd ever done any of the things Gerry had accused her of. Luckily Bob and Joanne had found a solution. Adopting a Korean baby had given them the child they'd longed to have, and Amy's arrival had alleviated Joanne's fears that Bob would leave her.

But maybe Joanne would hear this gossip. If she was acting strangely, as Bob had said, maybe she would react. Going up to Bob's closed door, Tracy knocked on it.

"How goes it?" asked Bob, looking up from the papers scattered over his desk top.

"Not well." Tracy closed the door and sank into the olive-green overstuffed chair Bob had found at a garage sale and installed in his cramped office. "We've got problems."

Putting down his pen, Bob leaned forward. "What kind of problems?"

"It seems you and I are the lovers of Dos Pueblos. The hottest item of gossip. Behind this closed door—don't ask me how, with so little room—a torrid affair has been evolving. And we're the last to know. Or at least I am."

"You're kidding," Bob laughed. "In here?" But he grew serious as he watched Tracy angrily comb her fingers through her hair, pushing it away from her eyes. "You're not kidding."

"I was just informed by our new principal that you and I are having an affair. Holmes told him." Tracy leaned forward. "You and I know it's a lie, but what if Joanne hears about it?"

Grasping the gravity of the situation, Bob sat back. "I'm not sure what she would say—especially right now. She knows how much you helped me when we were having problems, and she considers you her friend. I don't think she'd believe a rumor like that."

"If you don't mind," Tracy said, "this afternoon when I stop by I'm going to tell her what's being said. I'd rather get it out in the open. That way—"

"I nearly forgot," he interrupted. "We want you to stay for dinner—I'll barbecue some steaks. Joanne suggested it when I mentioned you might drop over." He nodded. "I think you're right. It would be better to tell her before she hears the gossip from someone else."

"Joanne will be the easy one to convince," said Tracy, knowing how much Bob's wife loved him. "The staff and students are going to be the hard ones."

"I suppose we'd better stop meeting in here." Bob glanced at the closed door and shook his head. "And at lunch."

"I don't think we have to cut off all contact!" Tracy thought back over the hours they'd spent together the past spring, especially while they were planning her Life class. "However, I guess we have been isolating our-selves from the rest of the faculty. We'll just have to make a point to mingle more." She rose to leave. "By the way, Prescott knows we tricked Holmes into approving the Life class."

"What did he say?"

"He wasn't pleased, but he's given me the go-ahead. I feel as if I'm on probation. He implied he's going to be watching me closely."

"Don't worry about Prescott," Bob said as she opened the door. "Everything will turn out fine. See you to-night."

Tracy stepped back into the hallway, closing the door behind her. It wasn't until she turned to leave that she noticed Mark. He was standing at the counseling files, but his eyes were on her.

"I . . ." Tracy began, glancing back at Bob's closed door. "That is, we were discussing what you'd told me earlier . . . about the gossip."

She paused, waiting for a comment, but he made none.

"Bob was as surprised as I was," she continued, feel-ing like a fox caught sneaking out of the chicken coop.

"I'm sure," Mark said, never breaking eye contact. "I can see why you were busy tonight. I thought you didn't mix business with pleasure."

"I don't," Tracy responded. "Tonight is strictly plea-sure. I'm having dinner at Bob's place—with his wife and daughter." She straightened her shoulders, deciding to play his game of stare down. Sapphire blue met dark brown. The atmosphere between them was charged with tension.

Mark's lips cynically curved into a faint smile. "A family affair. How nice." Shaking his head, he turned back to the file and resumed his search through the folders.

Tracy knew he didn't believe her. She wanted to grab his arm and order him to look at her—listen to her. Yet she knew it would be useless. Like Gerry, Mark had made up his mind. He would see the truth in his own fashion, and arguing would be futile.

3

THE EVENING OF ROSE'S PARTY the temperature was comfortably in the seventies. When Tracy stepped out of the shower she stood in front of her full-length mirror for a minute as she toweled herself dry. She'd finally lost the weight she'd gained at her mother's, and her figure was perfectly trim again. Dusting herself with a fragrant rose-scented powder, she remembered the way Gerry used to love to touch her smooth skin. It had been a long time since a man had touched her intimately. None of the men she'd dated since her divorce had aroused feelings even vaguely resembling passion. A good-night kiss was all she wanted or usually permitted. Sometimes, however, she did miss the sensations a loving caress could excite.

Those first few months she and Gerry were married had been good ones. She'd accepted his jealousy then, considered it flattering that he'd think other men would be attracted to her. He'd been her first lover, and had taught her how to please him. And oh, how she'd wanted to please him.

When she'd first realized Dr. Gerald White, her psychology professor, was interested in her, Tracy couldn't believe it. He was so much older, so mature and sophisticated. How could he find a nineteen-year-old sophomore interesting?

Yet he'd asked her out to lunch, then to dinner. He invited her sailing and took her to plays. Blond, good-looking and masterful, he was exactly the kind of man Tracy had dreamed of marrying. And when he asked her to be his wife, she didn't hesitate to say yes. Who could ask for more? He was intellectually stimulating and physically exciting.

She ignored her mother's arguments that Gerry was old enough to be her father. She attributed it to envy when her roommate warned her that any man who had been married twice before must have problems—and that Tracy hardly knew him. The day after he turned in her final grade they were married.

The fact that she was a virgin had surprised and pleased Gerry. Patiently he'd taught her the ways of love, and she'd gained confidence in her own sexuality. That was the beginning of the end.

Now that Tracy looked back, she realized Gerry had wanted her to remain the innocent, clinging girl he'd married. It was as she continued her education and matured emotionally that the problems began to emerge. First the jealousy, the irrational tirades if another man so much as looked at her. Then the verbal abuse, the constant put-downs.

At last she could take no more. When she accepted the job at Dos Pueblos, she already knew her marriage was on the rocks, but she stuck it out for six more months, trying to get Gerry to go with her for counseling. He'd refused. He had a doctorate in psychology and hadn't felt he needed counseling. So, despite the fact she'd sworn she would never get a divorce, she'd filed for hers on Valentine's Day. What had started as a dream ended as a nightmare.

With a sigh, Tracy hung her damp towel back on the rack, then slipped into lacy underwear. No use dwelling on the past. What had happened had happened. She would simply never repeat that mistake. When she married again, if she ever did, it would be to a mature, emotionally balanced man who could trust her and accept her as she was.

Stepping out of the bathroom into her spacious loft bedroom, Tracy went to her closet and pulled out a white cotton, surplice-wrap sleeveless dress with a deep vee neckline and wide black sash that matched the dress's jacket.

The problem was, she'd discovered, there were few single men who interested her. Most seemed to be either struggling with their own neuroses or wrapped up with the macho image. Maybe she'd studied too much psychology herself—it seemed like she spent most of her evenings either counseling her date or explaining why saying no to a man's proposition didn't mean she was frigid.

That's why she'd decided to go to Rose's party without an escort. George, her steadfast admirer from church, had let her down. After months of settling for a good-night kiss, the past weekend he'd come on like a beast. So much for him, thought Tracy, slipping the dress over her head and tying the sash.

A quick brushing smoothed her short hair back toward the nape of her neck, then she pulled a few strands in front of her ears. She swooped her long bangs across her forehead so they dropped casually over one eyebrow. It was a simple style; casual yet very feminine.

Her makeup was light: lipstick, a touch of blush,

mascara and eye shadow. Several times in her life she'd tried using more cosmetics to make herself look older—had even worn her hair in a more sophisticated style. But she'd never really felt comfortable with the result. She simply wasn't meant to be a slick glamour girl.

Inserting silver loop earrings and fastening a braided silver-and-black chain around her neck, she was ready. Tracy stepped into her high-heeled sandals and started downstairs.

Sam, her gray tiger cat, lifted his head from the pillow on the couch as she descended the wooden steps. As if knowing he'd be put out, he stretched and jumped to the floor, his tail arched proudly over his back as he strolled toward the glass door to the balcony.

"Don't chase the birds," admonished Tracy, leaning down to stroke his soft head before sliding open the door and letting him out.

She paused for a moment to watch the gulls dive after tiny crabs scurrying across the sand below. The sun was setting, turning frothy whitecaps to gold. Santa Barbara's sunsets often surprised people. The city was located along an east-west curve of the coast, so it seemed to the uninformed that the sun was setting in the north—not the west.

The cat jumped up on the railing of the redwood balcony. His green eyes focused on a sandpiper sprinting along the water's edge, and Tracy knew her warning would go unheeded. Her only consolation was that Sam rarely succeeded in catching a bird. Only the sick or foolish waited for his approach; perhaps it was the way of nature. Tracy closed the sliding door, picked up her purse, and left the house.

Rose lived in Montecito, the exclusive residential area east of Santa Barbara. Here resided the old rich—families who had had money for generations—as opposed to the nouveau riche who had built their homes in Hope Ranch Park. Huge estates and mansions were surrounded by wrought-iron fences and perfectly manicured lawns. Luxuriant with Spanish-style architecture, the elite area spread from the shoreline of the Santa Barbara Channel up the protective slopes of the Santa Ynez mountains. Palm, olive, fig and avocado trees lined the streets as well as the driveways. All around Tracy were adobe red and stucco white. Montecito was an artist's paradise and a haven for the wealthy.

Rose's father was in the diplomatic corp. If Tracy recalled correctly, he was now somewhere in South America. While her parents were away, Rose took care of the house—not that were was much to do. A cook did the cooking, a maid the cleaning and a gardener maintained the yard. Mostly Rose taught her five classes of Spanish—a second language to her—entertained and paid the bills. Not such a bad life, Tracy thought as she turned onto the Springers' driveway.

Walking up to the front door of the gracious two-story adobe, she could hear voices coming from inside. She was late and there were several cars parked in front of hers, but she noticed Mark's gray Mercedes roadster wasn't among them. Maybe he'd decided not to come. She knew he'd taken Rose out the night before, and she wondered how the date had gone. Knowing Rose, it was easy to conjure up a romantic scene. To Tracy's surprise, she found the image of Mark and Rose in a passionate embrace disturbing.

The maid answered the doorbell and Tracy stepped into the entryway, her heels clicking on highly polished blue-and-white mosaic tiles. "They're all out by the pool," the Mexican woman directed, taking Tracy's purse and jacket.

"Tracy!" Rose called from the portable bar set up on the patio between the house and the kidney-shaped swimming pool. "Over here."

Saying hello to Jeff Black and his wife, and nodding to several other teachers, Tracy walked over to where Rose stood.

"What would you like to drink?" Rose waved her long painted fingernails toward the bartender behind her. "I was just talking to Bill, here. He's a whiz on all the new concoctions."

"A plain, uncomplicated vodka collins for me." Tracy smiled at the man tending bar, and he nodded and reached for a tall glass.

"You didn't see Mark, did you? When you came in?" Rose glanced toward the door to the house, then took a sip of her frothy pink drink.

She was dressed in a figure-revealing black crepe-de-chine jump suit, with a halterlike front and nonexistent back. The dark silky material contrasted with her milky white skin, while diamond earrings glittered in her earlobes. Her red hair was swept back dramatically behind one ear and held by a diamond-studded comb. The effect was stunning. No wonder men fell at her feet.

"His car wasn't outside when I arrived," Tracy answered, taking the glass the bartender handed her.

"He said he'd probably be late." Rose slipped her arm through Tracy's and guided her to a corner of the patio, where they could talk in private. "I've got to tell you about last night."

"You had a good time?" Tracy knew by Rose's glow that she'd had a marvelous time.

"I'm in love. Mark Prescott is the most exciting man I've ever met."

"I think you also said that about Larry Harter last spring," Tracy said, grinning. Rose was always in love—or pining. She'd missed her calling when she'd chosen to teach Spanish instead of drama.

"This is different. First of all, remember I told you Mark's name sounded familiar? Well, guess who he is?"

"Who?" Her curiosity was piqued.

"None other than the son of Andrew Prescott. Mark's father is president of Prescott Industries, one of the largest oil companies on the West Coast. Our principal is probably worth millions."

"At least it explains that Mercedes sports car he drives," Tracy said, sipping her drink. "Why is he a high-school principal if he's loaded with money?"

"I asked him the same question. He said he likes working with young people, especially teenagers. He also mentioned starting a school of his own, when he has enough experience. I immediately volunteered my services," Rose said with a wink.

"I take it Prescott has a disciple."

Rose looked toward the house and lowered her voice. "Let me tell you, Tracy, last night was super, and if I have my way, tonight's going to be even better. He may not know it yet, but our dear principal's spending the night with me."

Tracy's eyes followed the direction of Rose's glance,

and she understood the smile curving her friend's sensuous lips. Mark had arrived. He paused a moment to glance over the crowd, then spoke to a couple standing near him.

Mark and Rose would make a perfect twosome, Tracy decided. They had similar backgrounds and probably similar interests. He certainly would never treat Rose as anything less than a mature woman, although he might be jealous of the way other men looked at her. Tracy knew that wouldn't bother Rose. She liked possessive men.

What upset Tracy was the effect Mark had on her. The mere sight of him caused her heart to race. It had happened twice at school when he'd showed up unexpectedly in her classroom, and it was happening again right now. She was reacting in a totally irrational manner, she told herself, letting her eyes travel from his thick wavy hair to his rust-colored corduroy blazer, plaid shirt and brown slacks. He always looked so damn handsome.

"Excuse me," said Rose, unaware of the effect Mark's presence was having on Tracy. "I'm going to see to it he gets a drink. Catch you later."

As Rose moved toward Mark, her hips swaying provocatively, Tracy frowned. Tonight Rose's blatant sexuality irritated her, though it had never bothered her before. She'd always enjoyed watching men fall over themselves for her redheaded friend. That Mark was attracted to Rose shouldn't disturb her. Why couldn't she simply ignore him?

For an hour Tracy tried. She wandered around the patio, sipping her drink and talking with the other teachers, their husbands and wives, many of whom she hadn't seen since the faculty Christmas party. She purposely avoided Mark, keeping her back to him as much as possible. Finally, her glass empty, she returned to the bar for a refill, and found Bob standing there.

"When did you get here?" Tracy asked. "Where's Joanne?"

"Home." For some reason Bob's grin reminded Tracy of a Cheshire cat. "She's still tired and now we know why."

"So, why?" Tracy set her empty glass on the counter. Whatever the reason for Joanne's constant exhaustion, from Bob's pleased expression it couldn't be serious.

"Remember that night you had dinner with us? You told Joanne she should get a complete checkup? Well, she did. And today she got the results."

Again he paused and Tracy had to prod him. "What did she find out?"

Bob put down his drink with a wide all-encompassing smile. "She's pregnant!" he announced. "After all these years and all those tests—she's actually pregnant!"

"Oh, Bob!" cried Tracy, hugging him and laughing in surprise. "I don't believe it."

Wrapping his arms around her, Bob held her close. "The doctor said it's not that uncommon. Once we got Amy, the pressure to have a baby was off and Joanne could relax and let nature take its course. They never could find a physical cause for her infertility. That's why she always felt so guilty, always blamed herself."

"I can't believe it!" repeated Tracy, stepping back to look at him. "What's Joanne say?"

"She can't believe it either, but she's happy. The doctor says she's eight to ten weeks along, so this tiredness shouldn't last much longer. She wanted to come tonight but just wasn't up to it; however, she insisted I come."

"Then let me buy you a drink," offered Tracy. "Especially since Rose is paying."

"Let's have champagne," Bob said, slipped his arm around her shoulders and affectionately drew her closer. "To celebrate."

"Champagne for two," she told Bill. After he'd handed them their glasses, Tracy clinked hers against Bob's. "Are you going to announce the good news tonight?"

"No, you're the only one Joanne gave me permission to tell." He was serious now, taking a sip of the bubbly wine. "I think she's afraid something might happen—you know, a miscarriage. The doctor said she's fine, but I promised I'd wait and not tell anyone but you until she began to show. So now that you know, you must promise not to tell anyone—least of all Rose."

Tracy laughed. "Rose would probably throw a baby shower next week if she knew."

She glanced across the patio toward their hostess. But it was Mark she noticed. He was watching her, frowning, and immediately Tracy felt uneasy.

She wondered how long he had been observing them, and what he had seen. An embrace. Two friends talking. No reason for her to feel guilty.

Tracy looked away and set down her champagne glass. There was music coming from inside the house. When she arrived, she'd noticed that the furniture had been moved, rugs taken away and the hardwood floor of the family room polished. A band was now playing. "Let's dance," she suggested.

She wanted to get away from Mark's eagle eyes. For four years she'd been harried by a jealous husband, had had to be so careful. Now she was a free woman, with no one to answer to but herself. And there was nothing between Bob and her but a wonderful friendship.

The band played several fast pieces, and Tracy quickly forgot her irritation as Bob and she imitated dance steps they'd seen the students do and improvised a few of their own. She was warm and breathless when the music changed to a slow romantic ballad. Ready to fall into Bob's arms, she was surprised to hear a deeper voice say, "My turn, Martin."

Tracy stiffened immediately as Bob stepped aside and Mark took his place. "Don't I have a say about whom I dance with?" she asked, holding herself back as Mark slipped his arm around her waist and took her hand.

"No." He pulled her closer, picking up the rhythm of the music and moving across the room, away from where Bob stood.

To make a scene would be ridiculous, but she wasn't about to throw herself into this domineering man's arms. Tracy's body was rigid, only her feet following his fluid motion.

"You look lovely tonight," he murmured, bending his head so that his breath stirred her hair.

"Thank you." Her reply was stiff. She would tolerate this dance, then walk away.

"I like your perfume."

"How nice."

"Do you have to resist every overture I make to be friendly?" he asked, turning her slowly, smoothly, until it seemed they'd become one with the music.

"Friends don't order, they ask." It was difficult not to forget her animosity and simply enjoy the pleasure of dancing with someone who could move so gracefully. Considering his size, it amazed her.

Suddenly he stopped and stepped away from her. The music continued and couples danced around them—fellow teachers who glanced at them with curiosity. Without letting go of her hand, Mark bowed. "Miss Dexter, may I have the pleasure of this dance?"

It was too ridiculous. Tracy laughed, willingly moving into his arms as he straightened to his full height. "You win," she said, chuckling. "And you look very handsome yourself."

"Thank you." He drew her closer, so her cheek rested against the ribbing of his jacket.

She could smell his cologne, its musky scent mixing with his clean masculine aroma. She wasn't about to tell him she also liked that. Her warmth blended with his and she felt flushed and light-headed. It was a good feeling, being held by Mark. He was strong, yet gentle. His lead was decisive and easy to follow. A tingle ran over her skin.

"Rose throws quite a party, doesn't she?" Tracy said, suddenly remembering Rose had told her she loved this man.

"Very nice," he murmured.

"She's done this every year since I started teaching." His hips were touching hers, his thighs brushing her skirt. She felt her muscles tighten. "Rose said you two had a nice time last night."

"We did." Mark moved his hand slowly over her back, his strong fingers gently kneading her shoulder blades. "Tracy, I don't want to talk about Rose."

"She's my friend," she tried to explain, wondering what Rose would say if she saw how closely they were dancing or knew the crazy, erotic thoughts running through Tracy's head.

"Is that why you've been avoiding me tonight? Look, I took Rose out to dinner. I didn't commit myself to her. If you'll recall, I also asked you out, but you refused."

"That was different," Tracy argued. "You were trying to prove a point."

"I asked you out because I find you very attractive."

Tracy gazed up at his face. He was watching her, smiling. Nervously she licked her lips. What would it be like to be kissed by this man?

"I . . . how do you like Santa Barbara?" she stammered, not certain if she liked the feelings Mark was arousing. Perhaps he didn't consider himself committed to Rose, but Tracy knew her friend was definitely interested in him and wouldn't welcome competition.

"Santa Barbara's charming. You're changing the subject, Tracy. What's the matter, are you afraid of me? Or is it Bob?" He glanced toward the edge of the room, where Bob was talking to Sylvia and her husband. "Your lover doesn't seem concerned."

Immediately Tracy pulled back, putting several inches between their bodies. "Bob is not my lover!"

"Come on, Tracy, I'm not blind." He gave her the space she wanted, but retained a firm hold on her waist. "Bob arrives by himself, you rush to his side and embrace. It's obvious what's going on. All I'm asking for is a chance. Consider this: unlike Bob, I'm single. There's no wife to hide from."

"You men are all alike!" Tracy fumed. "You see what you want, nothing more." She stopped dancing. "I've changed my mind, Mr. Prescott. I don't want to dance with you."

He let her go, and she was surprised that he did. Gerry would have made a scene.

Quickly Tracy walked out of the room and back to the patio. There were people gathered around the bar and around a table of food that caterers kept replenishing. Tracy wanted neither food nor drink. What she needed was time to be alone. Seeing a path leading from the patio into the garden, she took it.

She walked among neatly pruned rosebushes, oleanders, fuchsias and camellias until she was out of sight of the house. The scent of freshly cut grass lingered in the warm night air. Tracy filled her lungs with a calming breath and continued on down the cobblestone walk toward the stone wall that separated the Springer property from their neighbor's. Leaning against the cool rough surface of the waist-high barricade, she looked down the hill toward the lights of the city.

Behind her she could hear the music and laughter of the party. Somewhere in the distance a dog barked, and above her stars played peekaboo behind wispy clouds. There was a half-moon, its faint light giving her dress a ghostly appearance.

Dammit, if only Mark hadn't asked her to dance! She'd liked having his arms around her, the solid feel of his body—maybe she was getting desperate for a man. She'd heard that sometimes happened to women after their divorces. But why to her, tonight? And with Mark, of all people. He was her boss.

It had been one thing when he'd believed Holmes's lie about Bob and her. He hadn't known better then. But she'd told him it wasn't true, and he hadn't believed her. Tracy clenched her fists and stared out over the treetops toward the harbor.

"It's beautiful at night, isn't it," Mark said from behind her.

Startled, Tracy turned to face him.

"The small island—what's it called?" he asked, ignoring her surprised expression.

Looking back at the two Channel Islands silhouetted offshore, she answered, "San Miguel." Her voice was strained. He'd followed her after all.

But Mark seemed more interested in discussing the scenery than prolonging their argument. "Is San Miguel part of the Channel Island National Park?"

"All of the islands are—or will be in the near future. San Miguel used to be a bombing range and missile-tracking station."

"Ever been on it?"

He'd come closer and was standing beside her. Tracy tried to keep her voice level and ignore the wild beat of her heart. "Once. It's interesting. There's a foot trail across the flanks of two rounded hills, then you climb a deeply eroded ravine and come to a caliche forest. It's like stepping onto a lunar landscape. Plants that died thousands of years ago have been calcified. And if that's not eerie enough, some say the ghost of Juan Cabrillo, the Spaniard who discovered Santa Barbara, inhabits the island."

"Sounds fascinating. And the larger island?"

"Santa Rosa. It's a working cattle ranch, but someday

it will be bought by the federal government. There are Chumash Indian village sites and middens on both islands. Some of the sites on Santa Rosa suggest possibly the earliest presence of man in North America."

"You like history, don't you?" He was now looking out over the city.

"When it surrounds me like this, I do." It seemed Mark was calling a truce. Well, she was willing to go along. After all, she would have to work with the man for the next nine months. Deciding to show there was no animosity on her part, Tracy continued the topic. "I find it fascinating to live in a city that has been under the rule of three different countries. Santa Barbara is a blend of Spain, which established it, Mexico, which fortified it, and of course, the United States."

"You should teach a class in local history."

"Thanks, but no thanks." She grinned, her cheeks dimpling. "Phil Whitaker does that best."

Mark said nothing, his eyes focused on the lights below them. Tracy shifted her weight from one foot to the other, then wished she hadn't. They were standing so close the corded material of his jacket sleeve rubbed against her bare arm. A prickly sensation spread across her skin, and she tried to pull back inconspicuously.

Obviously he'd followed her out there, but it was doubtful that he merely wanted to discuss the landscape. Maybe he wanted to say he was sorry, to apologize for falsely maligning her reputation.

Tracy shivered, but not from the cold. Her nerves were on edge. Mark Prescott had a sexual appeal she couldn't ignore.

A breeze brought the scent of his cologne to her and

Tracy recalled their dance. She'd enjoyed being held by him—had been sexually aroused. For the first time in years she'd actually wondered what a man's kiss would be like, and wanted to know. Shyly she glanced up at his face to find him watching her.

"You're beautiful in the moonlight," he said huskily, turning toward her. "Hair the color of honey, eyes like sapphires."

"Mark, I—"

Lightly he placed a finger on her lips. "Don't say anything."

His fingertips glided over her face, tracing the contours of her delicate features. Mesmerized, Tracy obeyed his command. Neither of them said a word as they silently studied each other, memorizing every feature they could discern in the dim light.

His hand moved to her neck, gently massaging her tensed muscles. Tracy wasn't sure if she took a step toward him or if he pulled her closer. All she knew was that her hands were acting on their own, rising from her sides to touch the lapels of his jacket, to feel the ridges of soft corduroy.

His face was coming closer, those lips so inviting. One kiss wouldn't hurt, she told herself. This was merely to satisfy her curiosity, nothing more. She didn't want to hurt Rose, wouldn't do anything to hurt Rose, but . . . .

Tracy stood on her tiptoes, meeting him halfway.

They tasted each other, their lips moving together in a gentle exploration. He was delicious—warm, gentle and, "Oh-hh," she groaned, so persuasive. Her hands moved farther up his jacket until her arms were wrapped around his shoulders, her fingers combing through the thick hair at the nape of his virile neck.

Immediately he reacted, his hands coming down to her waist, and as he drew her hips against his, currents of excitement pulsed through her. This was not what she'd expected. Not this maelstrom of emotion that was suddenly overwhelming her.

He deepened his kiss, his tongue penetrating her mouth, challenging her into action. Daringly she met the invitation—her tongue carrying on a sensuous little duel with his.

In the back of her mind Tracy knew she should stop, should call a halt before things got out of hand. Her subconscious cried out a warning that this man was barely more than a stranger. He was principal of Dos Pueblos—the man Rose claimed to love.... But Tracy's entire being wanted to experience the sensations Mark was awakening, wanted to know the elemental pleasure he was igniting. Boldly she arched her body against his, all the while knowing her actions would arouse him even further. Pleasure was overruling reason.

He moaned a response, his breathing ragged, and his hands traveled slowly across her back until they reached her sides and the swell of her breasts. Within the confines of her bra each nipple hardened to a firm peak, and he grazed them with his thumbs, his fingers tightening around her rib cage. When he trailed kisses over her cheek and down her neck, Tracy trembled in his arms, alarmed by her response. No man had ever aroused her so quickly. Automatically she leaned back, exposing more of her throat.

Lightly he stroked the curve of her neck with one

hand, finding her wild and erratic pulse. He touched the edge of her dress, then teasingly moved his fingertips along the corded piping of her neckline, down to the valley between her breasts. The lower his fingers moved, the faster her heart beat, until she was sure he could feel it. Bending his head, he kissed the smooth, velvety skin above her breasts, every flick of his tongue searing her hot flesh.

Her dress was a pullover. There were no buttons to open, no zipper to undo. Tracy was sure if there had been, she would have eagerly exposed her breasts to his exploration, so complete was her submission.

His arm was a steel brace behind her back. She leaned against it and closed her eyes, groaning softly as the palm of his other hand flattened over her breast and began to move in slow, concentric circles. Her senses were reeling. Their hips were locked together, and she could feel his hard masculine contours through the fabric of her dress. There was no doubt she'd aroused his passions. No doubt within herself that he'd aroused hers.

Laughter sounded from the patio, a harsh reminder of where they were and whose house it was. Like a shock of cold water, reality forced itself through the haze in her brain. "No...oh, my God, no," she moaned, shaking her head and struggling to pull herself back from the depths of surrender. Opening her eyes, she wriggled to free herself from his embrace.

But Mark wasn't about to let her go. "Tracy," he groaned, gazing down at her flushed face. "You're so lovely. Like a flower. A rose as beautiful as any in this garden—"

"Rose!" Tracy cried. "Rose is one of my best friends...and she likes you. We can't be doing this in her backyard! I never meant...."

He silenced her with a deep probing kiss. Crushed against his body, held in his strong arms, she couldn't escape. For a moment she willed herself not to respond, tried to resist him, but with a faint whimper she finally gave in. As she returned his kiss, Mark's lips softened and his grip relaxed.

The fiery passion slowly ebbed, changing to a tenderness that was equally enjoyable. Finally he sighed and lifted his mouth from hers. "Don't feel guilty about Rose. You didn't start this, I did," he whispered.

"But I should have stopped you," she moaned, trembling as his hand stroked her bare arm. At the feathery caress she remembered how intimately she'd allowed him to touch her.

"Tracy." He reached up and cradled her face in his hands, tilting her head back so she had to look at him. "You couldn't have stopped what just happened any more than I could. Call it chemistry if you like, but we're attracted to each other."

"No!" cried Tracy, trying to shake her head but finding it impossible with his hands holding her prisoner.

Lightly he kissed her mouth, then the tip of her nose. A smile curved his lips as he looked down at her. "Face it, Miss Dexter, you can't keep your eyes off me any more than I can keep from watching you."

Tracy pushed herself free of Mark's hold, frightened by the truth of his statement. He'd seen her staring at him—knew he fascinated her. But it was wrong, all wrong! She wasn't going to be like her mother, making the same mistake, falling in love with the same type of man over and over. Maybe she'd made the wrong choice when she fell in love with Gerry, but she wouldn't be so foolish to repeat the mistake with Mark.

"I don't want to get involved with you," she stated. "I just can't."

"Why?" His smile faded as she backed away from him. "Because of Bob?"

That was the last straw. Perhaps Mark excited her— physically aroused her—but he was too much like Gerry. She'd been right. "Typical response," she said, feeling anger resolve her confusion. "Jump to conclusions and refuse to believe me. My reason has nothing to do with Bob. Look, you're my boss, and a man my best friend happens to be very interested in. I'm not getting involved with you...or with any man, for that matter. Now, if you'll excuse me—"

"Tracy!" Mark demanded, grabbing her arm as she started to walk away. "Either you're a very good actress or you felt something special just a while ago. Which is it?"

"It doesn't matter which it was!" Tracy jerked free of his grasp and hurried back to the house.

She hoped her hair didn't look too disheveled or her face too flushed. Her lips were bruised and sore and she moistened them with her tongue. Now she needed a drink—a strong one. The bartender raised a quizzical eyebrow when she ordered a straight shot of whisky and downed it. The heat of the liquor burned a path down her throat to her stomach and she choked, but at least it took away the taste of Mark's kisses. Her eyes stung with tears and she began to laugh, her voice holding a hint of hysteria.

"Are you all right?" asked Bob, leaving a group of teachers and coming to her side.

Tracy looked past Bob toward the garden, where Mark was just emerging onto the patio. "I'm fine—or I'll be fine in a minute." She coughed and took a deep breath. "Dance with me, Bob? Please."

He took her arm and they returned to the house. A slow song was being played and Tracy leaned against him, trying to sort through the confused feelings she was experiencing. It wasn't as good, dancing with Bob. He didn't have the sure strong lead Mark had. But it didn't matter. They were merely friends, not lovers.

Mark wouldn't believe that. He couldn't trust her, even though that was all she wanted from a man—trust and respect.

"What happened?" asked Bob. "You're as tense as a coiled spring."

"It's nothing I can't handle."

"Did Prescott do something? I saw him follow you outside."

"I don't want to talk about it," Tracy almost snapped.

For a few minutes they danced in silence. She was sorry she'd turned on Bob. He'd listened to her many times when she was trying to decide what to do about her marriage. Like a good psychiatrist, he'd let her do the talking, allowing her to work through her problems without giving advice. He was only trying to help her now.

"I'm sorry," she said when the music ended and they

walked to the side of the room. "I've just had a bad night."

"You know you can always talk to me, that I'll never say anything." He squeezed her hand.

"I know." She sighed, then leaned forward and kissed his cheek. "Thanks, but I just need some time to figure out what's wrong with me."

The band began another slow piece, but before they had a chance to move, Mark came up. "My dance," he said curtly, taking Tracy's hand and pulling her away.

"Haven't we been through this before?" fumed Tracy as he took her into his arms. "I don't want to dance with you."

"This isn't a social dance," he growled.

Tracy knew he was angry. Although he moved easily to the music, he did not attempt to hold her close, and the distance between them was more than physical.

"Are you trying to flaunt your relationship with Bob?" Mark demanded. "What kind of a woman are you?"

"Certainly not the kind you think I am." She was tired of defending her position.

"Is it your goal to break up his marriage?"

"Since Bob met me his marriage has improved." Let him figure that out, she thought smugly, feeling his fingers tighten around hers.

"You couldn't wait to get back into his arms. And to think I actually believed you in the garden! Your act of being concerned about Rose's feelings was very convincing—however, it doesn't seem to bother you that in Bob's case, you're taking another woman's man." His eyes were almost black as he glared down at her.

"I've taken nothing. Joanne and I share Bob. We each get what we need from him."

"How convenient. And I suppose she approves of the arrangement?"

"Completely." Tracy smiled, beginning to enjoy the deception. This was something she'd never been able to do with Gerry. There was a sense of adventure in feeding Mark's suspicions.

"And you're satisfied with the situation?"

"I am."

"You fool!" he growled, letting go of her. "Don't you realize you're messing up your life as well as his?" With that he walked away, leaving her stranded in the middle of the room.

"What was that all about?" Bob asked as Tracy rejoined him. They both turned to watch Mark stalk out of the room.

"That's called playing with fire. I'm probably going to pay dearly for my deception, but I enjoyed every minute out there. Someday I'll tell you all about it."

Respecting her wishes, Bob didn't press for an explanation. He took her in his arms and they finished the dance, talking about Joanne and his daughter, Amy.

Tracy felt she'd scored a victory, if only a personal one. She never would have been able to stand up to Gerry as she had to Mark. She was finally free of that old need to please an authority figure. But maybe she had gone too far. After all, Mark was the principal—her boss. What effect would their argument have on her future as a teacher?

There was another thing worrying her. Mark's kisses had thrown her totally out of control. She wasn't sure if it was him. Was she especially vulnerable this evening? Or was there, as he suggested, a special chemistry between them? Tracy wasn't sure, but she knew she'd have to be more cautious in the future.

She danced with Bob, then with a couple of other men—single teachers she'd been avoiding going out with ever since coming to Dos Pueblos. She stayed away from the patio because through the window she could see Mark was out there—with Rose.

The two, it appeared, were now inseparable. They were sitting at one of the pool-side tables talking, Rose gesturing dramatically with her hands, laughing and fluttering her long lashes. Tracy was sure she would get her wish—Mark would spend the night. What man in his right mind would turn down such an invitation? And from her experience in the garden, Tracy knew Mark was a virile male.

As the evening wore on, Mark's behavior in the garden infuriated her more and more. If he was so sure she was having an affair with Bob, why was he interested in her himself? Because he was certain she'd willingly go to bed with him? That she had no morals? Clenching her fists, she glared through the window. Rose was welcome to him.

Suddenly the party seemed frivolous and tiring. She found Bob, told him good-night, and whispered congratulations. Then she asked the maid for her jacket and purse. Something had happened tonight, something unexpected and unnerving. Tracy wasn't quite sure how to cope with it.

4

AFTER LEAVING THE PARTY, Tracy tried to analyze her feelings. Most of the night she lay awake, staring at the rough pine beams of her sloped ceiling, unable to understand why she'd reacted so wantonly to Mark's kisses. Every tick of the clock reminded her of the hour, forcing her to wonder jealously what he and Rose were doing now. If Mark was, indeed, spending the night at her friend's house.

By Sunday her mind wasn't any clearer. Even walking along the beach, with Sam strolling behind eyeing the birds, didn't ease her tension or erase her confusion. She was attracted to Mark—that was definite. Yet the scars from her divorce were still too fresh. She was wary of her own reactions.

Monday was a perfect example of Murphy's Law: anything that could go wrong, did. Just before leaving her house Tracy noticed a stain on the new dress she'd bought. That necessitated a quick change to her familiar red-and-white-striped cotton shirtdress. Then the film she'd planned on showing to her morning classes didn't arrive. At noon, as she was filling the duplicating machine, fluid spilled on two of her master dittos, and she spent most of her free hour retyping them. So when one of her sixth-hour students came to her desk and an-

nounced that Mr. Prescott had come to evaluate her,
Tracy wasn't really surprised.

She'd managed to go all day without running into
Mark, and as she looked up from her roll book, she
wished she could have extended that time. Her stomach
muscles constricted as he confidently strolled toward
her. He was the principal—her boss—yet when she
looked at him, it wasn't school matters but the memory
of his lips on hers that flashed through her mind. This
would never do.

"I've come to observe your Life class," Mark said,
stopping in front of her desk. "Anywhere in particular
that you want me to sit?"

"No, we're quite informal," she answered, gazing up
into his dark, brown eyes. Her voice was gravelly.
Quickly she cleared her throat and went on. "If you sit
in the circle you'll be expected to participate, but you're
welcome to join us."

He looked at the semicircle of chairs, the easel and
oversized pad of paper at one end. Students were
already gathering in the area, clustering in small groups.
"Not today," was his response. "Today I need to evaluate you and the class."

Trial by fire, she thought, standing as the bell rang. It
seemed ironic that he'd come this particular day. Today
she was beginning a unit on self-esteem, but at the moment she didn't feel at all confident. "Perhaps you'd like
to use my chair," she suggested.

"That would be fine."

Both of them were being so formal, Tracy almost had
to suppress a smile as she finished taking roll call and
marking the absentees. Who would think that they had

kissed each other with so much passion in a moonlit garden? *Forget it, Tracy Dexter,* she ordered herself as she walked to the door and clipped the absentee list into place.

When she picked up her notes, Mark had already moved her chair around to the front of her desk. He was seated, a clipboard with an official form on his lap, pencil in hand. Taking a deep breath, Tracy walked to the empty chair by the easel and sat down.

"Today we're going to study how other people's reactions affect your self-esteem," she began.

Then she made her mistake. She looked up—directly at Mark. His eyes were on her, boring mercilessly into her. *He doesn't believe me about Bob,* she thought. *No more than Gerry ever did, whenever I told him I wasn't having an affair. Mark might have been attracted to me Saturday night, but that's all it was—a physical attraction. He considers me immoral.* Tracy's eyes dropped to his hands, and she remembered the feel of his fingers on her breasts, their gentle, erotic caresses.

A flush of color covered Tracy's cheeks. This would never do. She had to keep her mind on teaching. "Everyone has a sense of self-worth," she began. "Name some of the positive and negative feelings people have about themselves."

Rising to her feet, Tracy went to the easel and marked down the responses the class gave. Then she broke the teenagers into smaller groups, and for fifteen minutes they role played—acting out various situations and responses, each student having an opportunity to participate.

Tracy would have liked to forget Mark, but that was

impossible. She was constantly aware of his presence in the room. Occasionally she would catch the movement of his pencil and her eyes would flick his way. He seemed so at ease, so confident. By contrast she was growing more and more nervous. What was he writing? Would Mark, like Holmes, consider this active method of teaching too radical?

"How did you feel when you were completely ignored?" Tracy asked, once the students were again seated in their chairs.

Answers flew, and her felt pen skimmed over the manila paper as she hurried to list each response. To her chagrin she misspelled a word, then dropped her pen. She glanced at Mark as she stooped to retrieve the fallen marker. *He must think I'm a klutz.* She sighed. *First the tea, and now this.*

"Our next exercise will be a contrast to the last one. This time I want you to practice active listening."

Tracy explained each of the steps, then separated the class into pairs. As one student talked, the other carefully listened, nodding and registering interest. Tracy moved around the room, observing and listening herself, and trying to keep her back to Mark as much as possible. Only when she returned to her easel and called a halt to the exercise did she glance his way.

He had stretched out his long legs, the soft flannel of his trousers outlining his muscular thighs. His brown corduroy jacket was unbuttoned and his light tan shirt and dark brown tie looked crisp and fresh, even after a long day. He was watching her, no sign of a smile, not even a nod of approval.

What am I doing wrong, she wondered. This method

of teaching wasn't new. Holmes lived in the past, believing every student should sit at a desk and face the front, but surely Prescott should be more up-to-date.

"How did you feel when your partner responded to what you were saying?" she asked the class, turning her attention back to the twenty-eight boys and girls. Again there was an immediate show of hands.

The dismissal bell rang before she'd been able to call on everyone. "Think about what we did today. Try the different methods and responses at home tonight and see what kind of a reaction you get," she called as the students clambered to their feet and began moving toward the door.

"Interesting," Mark said, standing up as she approached. "I see you don't have desks in here. I thought at the beginning of the year all the classrooms had desks."

"I had the custodian take them out and find tables and chairs," she answered. "He's looking for two more tables, but most of the time we either sit in chairs or the floor."

"Even in your sociology and psychology classes?"

"It works best for me. I like a relaxed atmosphere in my classes." She placed her notes on her desk and waited for him to deliver the familiar lecture on structured classrooms being better for learning. Her methods of teaching had upset Holmes. At the moment she wasn't sure what Mark Prescott thought. Maybe she'd made another faux pas.

He glanced at the clipboard in his hand, then at his watch. "I want to talk to you, but there's a student I have to see. Come to my office in twenty minutes."

His command was so formal Tracy wondered if he expected her to salute and click her heels, but all she said was yes. He left the room and she collapsed onto her chair, her heart hammering. It was so difficult to judge his response. He hadn't actually said he didn't like her teaching methods, but then, he hadn't expressed approval, either. His evaluation of her as a teacher was critical. He would be the one next spring who approved or disapproved her for tenure. If he disapproved she would be looking for another job.... Twenty minutes went by slowly, the tension mounting within her.

Locking her classroom door, she slung the strap of her leather purse over her shoulder, tucked a folder of papers she had to grade under one arm and started for the office. Her heels echoed in the empty hallway and butterflies fluttered in her stomach.

Rose was just leaving the school as Tracy turned the corner. "Ready to go?" she called, pausing at the door.

"I've got a meeting with Prescott," Tracy yelled back, motioning to the main office. "I don't know how long I'll be."

Rose nodded and let the door close behind her. Tracy watched the provocative swing of her friend's hips. She hadn't had a chance to talk to her since the party. The truth was, she hadn't wanted to hear her go on and on about her affair with Mark. "I'm jealous," Tracy sighed, disappointed in herself.

Entering the office, she smiled at Mrs. Baines. "I believe Mr. Prescott's expecting me."

"Come on in, Tracy," Mark called from his office, his door open.

She could see him at his desk, his head bent forward,

his right hand guiding a pen across a sheet of paper. From there she was looking directly at the top of his head—at his thick, sensuous hair. Slowly she approached his desk, taking in a deep breath. *This man is the principal. I can't always be thinking about his looks*, she silently lectured herself.

"Sorry to keep you late," he apologized, not even bothering to look up. "Are you doing anything this afternoon?"

"No." She stopped in front of his desk, but didn't sit down.

"Good." With a flourish he signed his name, glanced over the paper, then folded it and slid it into an envelope. "Then you won't object to riding into Santa Barbara with me. I have to deliver this to the superintendent's office, but I also want to discuss your evaluation while it's fresh in my mind."

He stood, slid the envelope into his breast pocket, then picked up the clipboard with evaluation form attached. Before Tracy could think of a reason why she couldn't go with him, he'd come to her side and slipped his hand under her elbow, guiding her toward the door.

"I'll see you tomorrow morning, Mrs. Baines," he told the secretary.

He didn't hold the car door for her, and Tracy was slamming hers shut as he turned the key in the ignition. "Look this over," he ordered, handing her the clipboard. "That is, if you can decipher my notes. If you disagree with anything I've put down, we'll discuss it before I have Mrs. Baines type the final copy."

His writing was hurried but legible. Quickly she

scanned the evaluation form, then slowly read each item and his response.

Appearance: Attractive...neatly   groomed... dress's bright color a good touch.

Preparation: Excellent. Room set up before class.

Presentation of Material: Nervous. Probably because I'm here.

"I'm afraid I was quite nervous," she confessed. "I felt like a student teacher this afternoon. You know, Mr. Holmes only evaluated me once last year. Even then he didn't stay more than ten minutes."

"I gather from talking to others that Holmes wasn't the best principal in the district." He glanced her way before pulling the sleek sports car onto the freeway, a smile tugging at his lips.

Tracy laughed and relaxed a bit. "He was the worst, as far as I'm concerned."

Mark said nothing, and she let the subject drop. Gossiping about Holmes wouldn't be appropriate, and she sensed this man didn't engage in back stabbing anyway. Her attention returned to the evaluation sheet.

Content of material: Good. Exactly what these students need. Certain to develop awareness and better communication skills.

Response of students: Excellent. Everyone participated. Students enthusiastic.

Comments: Obviously Miss Dexter has done a great deal of research in this area; however, the lesson ran too long. Homework assignment given too hastily. Possibility that some students didn't hear or understand.

"You're right," she nodded.

"About what?"

"That I need to pay more attention to the clock. I get so involved with what's going on I sometimes forget the time, and the bell rings before I've finished."

"Not such a bad quality. I'd rather see that than a clock watcher. Assign a student the responsibility of warning you five minutes before the bell."

She read on. There were a few other remarks, all complimentary. "I'm surprised," Tracy said at last, looking up. "This evaluation is certainly better than I'd expected."

"What *did* you expect?" Again he glanced her way, a full smile curving his lips. "You know you're a good teacher. You wouldn't have dared schedule such an innovative class if you hadn't thought you could teach it. Not that I fully agree with the way you handled the matter, but in this case the end does seem to have justified the means."

"Thank you."

"I will, however, be dropping in on the class from time to time to see how you're handling the various units. I've looked over your lesson plans for the year, and there are a few areas where I may get calls from parents. I want to know exactly what's going on in that classroom."

"You're always welcome," she said, studying him with a new sense of appreciation. She had to admit he was right to be concerned. Even in this day and age there were parents afraid of exposing their sixteen- and seventeen-year-olds to information about drugs or sex. To Tracy it was like burying your head in the sand, and she hoped she could convince those parents who did object that knowledge was far safer than ignorance.

"I didn't put everything I should have into that evaluation," Mark said seriously.

What had he left unsaid? Once again Tracy looked over the categories.

"I didn't put down how pretty you are," he answered, as if she'd spoken aloud. "I could have gone on for a page about the color of your eyes, another on how delectable I find your lips."

"Mr. Prescott!" She stared at him, and he grinned.

"That's right, you don't like to mix business with pleasure, do you. Then let me simply say, I'm quite impressed with you, Tracy Dexter." He turned the car off the freeway and drove along the tree-lined streets of downtown Santa Barbara. "In fact, we can discuss how impressed I am over a drink, as soon as I've delivered these papers."

"I don't think we should." A drink was the last thing she needed. "What if someone should see us?"

"It's not against the law for a principal to buy a teacher a drink after school hours," he laughed, pulling into the district-office parking lot.

"I have papers to grade. I've got to get home." She was searching for an excuse, any excuse. Even now, sitting so close to him, she could feel the magnetism.

Alcohol might lower her defenses, and it was clear she needed her wits around this man.

"One drink won't take that long. Besides, I have something else I want to discuss." He opened the car door.

"What?"

Winking, he slid out of the car. "That I'll tell you over a drink. I'll be just a minute."

With long ground-eating strides, he left her and disappeared into the one-story Spanish-style office building. Tracy leaned back in her seat and sighed. Mark Prescott was a very determined man! As she waited, she reread the evaluation form. His comments clearly showed he understood what she was trying to achieve with the Life class. That pleased her. Holmes would have seen nothing but chaos. But then, Mark had shown in many ways that he was nothing like Edward Holmes.

Palm trees lined the parking area, their fronds rustling in the breeze. The air was warm and she inhaled its salty aroma, feeling pleasantly relaxed. She should be adamant, should absolutely refuse to have a drink with him. But deep down she knew she would capitulate. If she was truthful, she would admit the idea of spending more time with Mark excited her. There was a definite sexual tension between the two of them—she could feel it. Like two magnets they were drawn together, on one level anyway. On another she was resisting.

A smile played on her lips. Mark didn't seem the least bit hesitant about flirting with her. So, he considered her pretty. Instead of being irritated, she found his comment flattering. Her ego was still suffering from the cutting remarks Gerry had made during their divorce. It was nice to know a handsome, obviously experienced man found her attractive.

Mark came out of the building, the wind blowing his hair back from his face, giving him a rugged, energetic appearance. Tracy sighed. There was definitely a physical chemistry between the two of them. It was going to be difficult to resist his charm, but resist she must.

"So much for business," he said, settling himself into the car. "The El Paseo okay with you?"

"Mark, I really don't think—"

"Good, it's one of my favorites, too." He started the car, totally ignoring her protest.

With a smile, Tracy reconciled herself to having a drink with him. Lack of persistence was certainly not one of Mark Prescott's faults.

Pueblo Viejo—old town—was the fourteen-block area around city hall, where buildings were required by law to follow the Spanish-Moorish style of architecture. Although the Mediterranean style was predominant in many of the buildings throughout Santa Barbara, going downtown was like stepping into the past. County courthouse, library, museum, restored houses, theater—everywhere they went tourists could see picturesque adobes with red-tiled roofs and fancy iron grille work. And around the buildings were lush green lawns, beautiful flower gardens and a variety of trees, both native and imported. To all who came to the city of Santa Barbara, the downtown core was a reminder of bygone days.

Mark parked in the heart of Pueblo Viejo and led the way across State Street to the El Paseo, a shopping arcade reminiscent of Old Spain. Two narrow walkways guided shoppers past art galleries and charming import and specialty shops, then converged on an open patio, which contained a sidewalk cafe, a fountain and the dining courtyard of the El Paseo resturant. Mark guided Tracy inside.

A hostess seated them at a corner booth in the cocktail lounge. Tracy tried to ignore the quickening of her pulse as Mark slid in next to her, his arm lightly touching hers, but it was difficult to disregard his presence. The soft flannel of his trousers brushed against her bare leg, and she shivered slightly. Suddenly the atmosphere seemed very intimate, and she wished she'd been more determined in her refusal to have a drink with him. It was going to be very difficult to keep him from seeing how he affected her.

At first she considered ordering something nonalcoholic, then decided that might make Mark ask questions, bring attention to her nervousness. After all, he'd seen her drinking at Rose's. "I'd like a margarita," she said when the waiter arrived.

"May I see your ID, miss?" the man asked politely but firmly.

Mark chuckled softly under his breath.

Flustered, Tracy fumbled in her purse, trying to find her driver's license. "I'm twenty-five years old!" she fumed, at last handing him a plastic folder.

"You are lucky to look so young, miss," the waiter said with a smile, returning her license. "And what would you like, sir?"

"A margarita sounds fine." Mark was still grinning when he leaned back and stretched his arm out on the seat back behind her.

"You think it's funny," stormed Tracy, stuffing her belongings back into her purse. "All my life I've been taken for younger than my age! It's not always an advantage."

"Someday you'll be glad you look young."

"I've also heard that one a thousand times!" Irritated, she slammed her purse down on the red velvet cushion.

"I don't seem to be picking the right words." Mark shook his head. "Tracy, the reason I asked you to come with me this afternoon is that I want a chance to apologize."

"Apologize?" Her eyes turned a darker blue in the dimly lit lounge, her pupils wide with amazement as she tried to imagine why he'd want to apologize. She'd never received a more honest and comprehensive evaluation. "I'm flattered by what you said about my teaching. I was so nervous this afternoon, I was certain you'd have a list of complaints."

"You're an excellent teacher," he said softly. "The students speak highly of you, and so does the faculty. No, what I want to apologize for is my behavior Saturday night."

Quickly Tracy looked away. That was one topic she wanted to avoid. The less said about Saturday night the better.

The waiter brought their drinks and Mark paid the man before saying, "Rose told me about Bob and you...how you've helped him. I acted like a fool, Tracy, accusing you of having an affair and then refusing to believe you when you told me I was wrong."

"Yes, you did." She reached for the long-stemmed glass and touched her lips to the salty rim. Purposefully she avoided his eyes. She'd been through this scene before. Not with Mark, but with Gerry. How many times had he begged her forgiveness when he'd discovered his accusations were false? Over the years she'd lost count.

Noting her cool response, Mark went on, "Of course, you didn't help matters Saturday night. You deliberately suggested a ménage à trois."

"I did not!" she flared. "It was you and your dirty mind suggesting a three-way love affair. I said Joanne and I both got from Bob what we needed—and that's the truth. Bob's given me a great deal of good advice the past two years. He's my friend!" She punctuated her statement with another gulp of her drink.

"Tracy, what can I say? If Holmes hadn't suggested—"

"If you had believed me in the first place," she interrupted, "there wouldn't be anything to say. But no, you had to run to Rose and ask her."

"Rose thinks the world of you."

"And I like Rose," she returned. "In fact, I have several friends. Would you like their names so you can check out my story with each of them?"

"Tracy, you're making too much of this."

"Am I? You're the one who started it, Mr. Prescott." She finished her drink. "Let's change the subject."

"All right," he said, "have dinner with me tonight. We can eat here, or go anywhere you'd like."

"No." This time she was firm. "I told you before, I'm not going to go out with you. Now, if you don't mind, I'd like to leave. I have a stack of papers to grade tonight, and the sooner I get started the better."

"Would you go out with me if I was merely a teacher and not your principal?"

"No." Playing with the stem of her empty glass, she avoided looking at him. "I've refused dates from teachers." That was one thing she'd decided when she divorced Gerry—never again would she fall in love with a teacher.

"Why?"

"I have my reasons." A glance his way momentarily made her question those convictions. Mark Prescott was without a doubt the most attractive man she'd ever met—and the most exciting. A definite "catch," as Rose would put it.

"And I take it you're not about to reveal those reasons?" His eyebrows rose quizzically.

"Correct." Despite her physical reaction, Tracy knew she had to avoid this man. There was her fear of repeating her experience with Gerry...and there was Rose. "Please, take me back to my car," she insisted.

He frowned, then lifted his glass and drained his drink in one long gulp. Standing, he pulled the table forward so she could slide out. Together, in an icy silence, they retraced their steps to the car.

As he drove back toward Goleta, and the outskirts of Santa Barbara, neither of them spoke. Tracy stared out the side window, pretending to study the landscape. The truth was she barely noticed when they passed the Earl Warren Showgrounds, or how the late-afternoon sun was turning the mountain slopes to gold.

The Santa Ynez range formed a majestic shield around Santa Barbara, sheltering it from winds and storms, just as the Channel Islands formed a protective barrier against the ocean's turbulence. The result was a city of postcard beauty. "La Tierra Adorado"—the beloved land—was what the early Spaniards had called the area. But Santa Barbara's beauty was lost on Tracy this afternoon. Jumbled, confused thoughts—about Mark and her reactions to him—occupied her mind.

When they pulled into the school parking lot, it was empty except for her white Mustang and the custodian's red, white and blue van. The young man would be somewhere in the building, sweeping out classrooms, his portable radio blaring out a popular rock song.

Tracy turned to retrieve her folder from behind her seat, then gasped as Mark's hand wrapped around her wrist. He shut off the car engine and faced her. "We need to talk."

"Let me go!" She tried to ignore the intensity of his gaze, but a shudder ran through her body.

"The other night you responded to me. If I hadn't been so stupid about Bob and you, everything would be fine now."

"No, it wouldn't," she insisted. "Mark, you're the principal of this school and you're having an affair with my friend. I don't want to get involved with you." With a twist she tried to pull free of his grasp.

"My position as principal should have nothing to do with us. And I am not having an affair with Rose."

"You deny you spent Saturday night with her?" Tracy stopped struggling briefly.

"Did she tell you that?"

"No." Tracy realized suddenly that she hadn't. "But when I talked to her at the party she was certain you'd stay. And when you went to her after leaving me that night, I assumed...."

"That I would kiss you in the garden, then sleep with

Rose? I won't claim to be celibate, Tracy, but I do have morals. Although Rose is a very beautiful woman, I find you far more intriguing." He reached out with his free hand and brushed her cheek with the backs of his fingers.

Immediately she pulled away. "Why? Because you thought I was having an affair with Bob?"

"No." He frowned. "In fact, that bothered me more than I like to admit. I can't tell you how relieved I was when Rose assured me you weren't involved with Bob." Half closing his eyes, he sighed. "To tell you the truth, I was jealous."

Jealousy. Oh, how she hated that word. It had always been Gerry's response. But was she any better? If they were being honest, she'd been jealous of Rose. It shouldn't matter whom Mark dated—or slept with—but to her dismay, it seemed to.

She was remembering her miserable weekend, the torture she'd put herself through, when Mark leaned forward. Tracy's eyes locked with his, and her heart began to thud. *No!* she wanted to say. *You mustn't kiss me . . . can't take the chance.* But no words came out.

His hand slipped behind her head to slowly draw her closer, and Tracy reached over to rest her hand on his shoulder. She did want him to kiss her. She'd wanted it ever since he'd walked into her classroom that afternoon.

Gently, persuasively, his mouth moved over hers, his lips still salty from the margarita. A heady feeling came over her—one that Tracy knew had nothing to do with the drink she'd had. She'd been fine until now. No, it was Mark. He was the reason she couldn't think straight.

Damn, he's lovely, she thought, her mouth yielding to his tender, compelling persistence. She'd always thought Gerry was an expert in the field of kissing, but by comparison he had been an amateur. *No, Mark, you're no celibate*, she silently agreed as each kiss became more intoxicating.

His tongue probed her lips, and she willingly parted them. A warm pulsing sensation raced through her veins. How easy it was to give in to the exhilaration, drink in the taste and smell of him. Like an aphrodisiac, his drugging kisses were weakening her resistance.

"There's something very special about you, Tracy Dexter," he sighed at last, lifting his mouth to lightly graze her cheek with his lips. "I wanted to call you all last weekend, but I was out of town. So I had to console myself with memories—wonder if I'd exaggerated our kiss in the garden or if you really were this warm and responsive."

"Mark, Saturday night was a mistake. This is a mistake," she argued weakly. But once again his mouth covered hers, silencing any further protests.

For one brief moment, when his hand touched her breast, she tensed, her pulse jumping at the contact. Then she relaxed, closing her eyes and letting a new wave of erotic feelings flow over her.

Mark was doing everything right. There was no rush to his actions, no fumbling, no groping. When one nipple had hardened to an aching peak, pressing against the confines of her bra, he gently began on the other one. Long before he began to loosen the buttons of her dress, she craved his hand on her burning flesh. As he released the front clasp of her bra and cupped her breast he reverently breathed her name. Blindly she reached out to undo his shirt. Trembling fingers touched the mat of brown hairs on his chest.

Caught in a whirlpool of emotions, Tracy leaned back against the car seat. His thumb and forefingers gently squeezed her nipple, inflicting a savage-sweet pressure, and she groaned. Lower in her body desires she'd suppressed for months flamed to life. Mark kissed her neck, finding the sensitive hollow of her throat, and her fingers splayed out across his rib cage. Dear God, he knew how to arouse her.

She was breathing hard when he removed his hand from her breast. Her lids fluttered open and she reached up to run her fingers through his thick wavy hair. Although he said nothing, his sensuous downward gaze told her of his desire. She was experiencing the same need. With a slight pressure she drew his head down, then sighed in pleasure as his lips surrounded an aching nipple.

Again she closed her eyes, reveling in the exquisite sensations spiraling through her body. His tongue teased, soothed, aroused, every touch bringing delight. Her own reaction was unabashed, almost hedonistic.

Then his hand slid down over her hip, his fingers slipping around to her bottom. A gentle squeeze and she was burning with desire. His lips sought hers and she arched her back. They were both gasping for breath when Mark reluctantly withdrew his mouth.

"Honey, you're driving me wild," he groaned. "But it's too risky here in the school parking lot. Let's go to my place. We can come back for your car later."

His passion-filled eyes devoured her, and Tracy knew he was struggling for control.

Frightened as she was by her own needs, her voice was shaky. "No, Mark, I won't go with you! We've got to stop. I never should have let you kiss me...touch me."

"Why do you insist on denying what you feel?" he demanded, his gaze darkening.

"Because I know nothing can come of the two of us." Jerking free of his grasp, she turned her back to him. Why had she allowed things to go so far? She trembled, afraid of giving in to her own physical desires.

"You want me as much as I want you. Admit it," he growled.

"Sure, I'll admit you turn me on," she cried, refusing to look at him. "You're a good-looking man and you know all the right moves. But that's not enough."

"What do you want? A proposal?"

"Don't be ridiculous." Her fingers fumbled with the clasp of her bra. "I was married to a man like you. I'm certainly not going to repeat that mistake."

"You hardly know me."

"I know enough about you." Angrily she rebuttoned her dress.

Turning back to face him, she noticed he hadn't moved, that his shirt was still opened, his tie askew. But the look of desire was gone from his eyes, replaced by confusion. Swallowing hard, she tried to make her point clear. "Mark, be sensible. You're the principal—my boss. You warned me about Bob. Can't you imagine the gossip that *we* would stir up?"

"This is different. I'm not married."

"It doesn't matter. I'm not getting involved with you. I've said it before, and I mean it."

"Is there someone else?"

"I don't believe it!" she cried, pressing her palms to her temples. "No, there's no one else. You can ask Rose, if that will help convince you." Tracy reached for her folder. "My divorce was final last year. For the first time in years I'm my own woman. I simply don't want to get involved—not with you, not with anyone. That's all."

He said nothing as she picked up her purse and opened the car door, but his hand caught her arm, stopping her before she slid out. "I don't understand you, Tracy. You're an intelligent woman. What we just shared was special, and you know that."

"What we shared was sexual," she sighed. "Yes, it was good, but I've learned that's not enough. There has to be a lot more between two people."

"And there can't be more between us?"

"No."

"You're still upset because I didn't believe you about Bob."

"That and other things." She felt sorry for him in a way, he looked so dejected. But then she remembered how Gerry had always assumed a doleful expression when he tried to make up. She would forgive him, then days or weeks later he would repeat his jealous outrage, accusing her of having a lover if he saw her as much as talking to a man.

"Give us a chance, Tracy! Let me take you out. If you don't want to get sexually involved right now, I can wait. I'm a patient man."

She shook her head and looked down at his hand, which was still on her arm. "I won't go out with you," she said. "You can hold me here as long as you like, but I'm not going to change my mind."

Slowly he released his grip, then dropped his hand. "I don't know what you want," he said at last.

"A chance to be me." Tracy stepped out of the car, then paused to call back. "Thanks for the drink and for all the nice things you said about me in that report."

"I meant them." His eyes followed her as she went to her car.

When she drove out of the parking lot, the Mercedes was still parked in the same spot, and from her rearview mirror, Tracy could see Mark seated behind the wheel. A part of her wanted to go back, to discover the heights of pleasure she knew he could bring, but reason stopped her. Gerry had given her sexual pleasure and emotional pain. The latter had outweighed the former. It was better to put an end to her relationship with Mark before she was hurt again. The question was, could she?

5

It was December, and a light rain was falling as Tracy drove into the high-school parking lot. Her headlights illuminated only a few cars and she swung into a spot near the gym. The dance wouldn't begin for a half hour, but she wanted time to shed her coat and find a good spot to stand.

Turning off the car's lights, she pulled the keys from the ignition and dropped them into her purse. She hadn't brought an umbrella. Somehow the rainy season always caught her by surprise. The school year seemed to be flying by.

Pulling her tan raincoat close and holding up the hem of her dress, Tracy hurried through the drizzle to the main entrance of the gym. Bob saw her coming and held the door open.

"Wouldn't you know it would rain tonight," she exclaimed.

"At least it's not a hard rain," he said, helping her with her coat.

With a swipe of her hand Tracy brushed a few droplets of water from her cheek. Then she shook her head, her bangs falling casually into place above her eyes, the light above illuminating the golden hue of her hair. Her dress was a red crepe, with puffy full-length sleeves and a scooped neckline. A softly gathered skirt flared out gracefully from the fitted waistline, the silky material falling gently around her ankles above delicately strapped matching red heels.

"Am I the last one here?" she asked, glancing around the gymnasium and seeing several other members of the faculty.

"Rose and Mark haven't arrived yet." Bob hung her coat on the rack, then offered his arm. "Madame, may I escort you in?"

"With pleasure," she smiled, hooking her elbow through his.

But inside Tracy was not as lighthearted as she acted. Bob's remark about Rose and Mark had brought a quick pang of jealousy. It seemed that Mark was spending a great deal of time with Rose lately. And Rose was being especially secretive about what they were doing. That surprised Tracy. Rose was generally quite open about her love affairs. Perhaps it was Mark's position. Or perhaps this time it was serious.

Tracy realized she had no claims on Mark. Any she might have had she'd forfeited that afternoon in the parking lot. No, she didn't even have the right to be jealous. She'd told him she wasn't interested, so why shouldn't he turn to Rose.

"How's Joanne doing?" Tracy asked, trying to get her mind off Mark.

"She's starting to show, and looking more beautiful every day," he beamed. "She wanted to come tonight, but was afraid three hours on her feet would be too much."

"That plus the volume of the music." The band was

beginning to tune up. Tracy covered her ears as a loud squeal emanated from the speakers. "It would be terrible for your baby to suffer a hearing loss before he was born," she yelled.

"So you're sure the baby will be a boy, too."

"Why not? Little Amy needs a brother." Tracy stopped in the center of the gym and slowly turned around, admiring the work of the decorating committee.

The Christmas dance was always a joy to chaperon. It was one of the few times during the year that the students dressed up and decorated the gym. The school's artificial Christmas tree had been set up in one corner—red and white lights, with ornaments and garlands picking up the evening's color theme. Gigantic white snowflakes of painted cardboard covered with glitter were suspended from the ceiling and were turning slowly above their heads, while twisted ribbons of red and white crepe paper covered the usually drab gray walls.

In one corner a white linen cloth was draped over a cafeteria table, concealing its scratched and ugly metal legs. A large bowl filled with red punch had been placed in the center and was surrounded by small plastic cups, red-and-white napkins and platters of sugar cookies. Two girls in party dresses and tiny white aprons fussed over the arrangement, nervously glancing toward the entrance doors.

Faculty members usually tried to be as inconspicuous as possible at school dances. They were there in case of emergencies, to check bathrooms for smoking and to patrol the parking area. Tracy didn't mind spending a

Friday night watching others enjoy themselves. Young love was a delight to observe.

The Christmas dance was formal—couples only—and Tracy always enjoyed seeing who came with whom. Some students were obviously on their first date, awkward in their shyness. She could still recall her own first date, the punch she'd spilled on the boy's suit and the cleaning bill her mother had received the following week. Tracy smiled. She'd always been a klutz when she was nervous, though eventually she'd learned to relax when she was out with a man.

Most of the time she'd gone to dances because they were parties, not because there was a romance involved. When she was seventeen, however, a romance had developed. She had dated Glenn most of her senior year in high school. When they went to dances, they had clung to each other, sneaking kisses in the shadows and forgetting anyone else existed. It had been puppy love, but at the time Glenn had been her whole world. For that reason she always took the romances of her students very seriously.

The outside door opened, and Tracy looked up.

Rose entered first, with Mark behind her, closing a large black umbrella. Rose looked stunning in a sophisticated floor-length gown of shimmering kelly green satin. Thin straps held up a fitted bodice, a small vee at the center accenting her deep cleavage and bringing attention to her full bust. The cummerbund-style sash made her tiny waist look even smaller, while the skirt reflected the light and turned Rose into a living Christmas delight.

And Mark was the man who would receive her gifts,

thought Tracy, her eyes turning to him. He looked the perfect escort in a black tux, pleated white shirt and black tie.

It was impossible not to stare at him. For three months she'd tried to overcome the attraction she felt, had hoped familiarity would make it easier to ignore him. But time only seemed to increase his appeal.

He hadn't asked her out again, hadn't even appeared interested, but he was visible every school day and impossible to avoid. It wasn't uncommon for him to drop in on one of her classes and stay a while. She'd heard other teachers mention he was doing the same with them. True to his word, Mark Prescott was actively involved with the workings of the school.

And the students respected him, even though not all of them liked him. Infractions of school rules were not tolerated, and Mark's punishment was swift. It was soon known that Mr. Prescott didn't hesitate calling parents—sometimes taking them away from their work for a conference—or suspending students from school. Tracy couldn't remember when Dos Pueblos had ever run as smoothly, and the rest of the faculty raved about the changes in the classroom atmosphere.

"They make a good-looking couple," Bob said, and Tracy jerked her eyes away from Mark guiltily. In her reverie she'd forgotten Bob was there.

"Rose told me she's getting to know our principal quite well," Bob went on. "Think there's a wedding in the offing?"

A knot gripped Tracy's stomach as she glanced back to see Mark lean toward Rose and whisper something in her ear. Rose grinned and nodded, then touched his arm before walking toward the Christmas tree.

"I don't want to discuss Rose's personal life," Tracy said. Then she quickly added, "I'm sure Rose would tell us if she wanted us to know. Well, I think I'd better find a discreet spot to position myself. The kids will be coming soon. I'll see you later."

In a corner of the gym where the lights were low, Tracy found the spot she wanted. From this vantage point she could watch the dancers as well as those on the sidelines.

The students were already arriving, looking like models from fashion pages: the girls in makeup, long dresses and new hairstyles; the boys in rented tuxedos, their faces scrubbed and, where possible, shaved. Intrigued by the parade, Tracy didn't notice Mark's approach.

"They look like different people, don't they," he chuckled. "Amazing what clothes can do."

"Isn't it?" She stared at Mark and swallowed hard. His tuxedo accentuated his broad shoulders, its rich black color making his hair and eyes appear even darker. A red carnation was inserted in his buttonhole, and in his hand he held a corsage of red and white carnations.

"The dance committee asked me to present you with these flowers," he said, noting her glance. "May I pin them on you?"

"You don't—" she began, but she was too late. Mark reached forward, his fingers sliding under the neckline of her dress. He lifted the material slightly, his fingertips brushing against the rise of her breast. Then, holding the corsage in place, he deftly pushed a pin through the stem. It was done in an instant, but the effect lingered on. Tracy stared at him, her mouth still open, the words failing to come.

Her skin tingled where he'd touched her, a warm rush of blood coursing through her veins. For Tracy there was no one in the room but the two of them. His gaze met hers, and an energy flowed between them that warmed and excited her. His lips were inviting, and she wanted to step into his arms and taste the sweetness of his kisses.

"You look lovely tonight," he said, his voice far too husky to be normal.

"Thank you," she murmured. Time had changed nothing. Whatever his relationship with Rose, the attraction between them was still there. *He wants me as much as I want him,* Tracy realized, her heart thudding in her ears.

"Mark!" Sylvia Johnson called above the noise of the band as she approached the two of them. "Could you bring in the other coatrack?"

"Right away." Mark glanced toward the door, where the first rack was nearly filled with rain-spotted wraps. Then he lightly ran his fingertips along the silky material of Tracy's sleeve. "I'll see you later."

"Don't the girls look pretty, all dressed up," Sylvia stated as Mark walked away. Her own white taffeta evening suit made a striking contrast against her bronze-colored skin. "Wouldn't you love to see them wear dresses every day?"

Tracy smiled at the counselor. "I'm afraid in my classes it wouldn't work out very well. Half of the time we end up sitting on the floor, and I'm glad to see the girls in jeans."

"Oh well, I suppose it was just an idle thought." Sylvia laughed. "My own daughter has a fit if I suggest she wear a dress more than twice a week. It's so different from when I went to school. Jeans were forbidden then, for boys as well as girls, and all schools had dress codes. I guess times change. One thing that hasn't changed is the smoking, however! I'll see you, Tracy. I want to check the girls' bathroom."

Tracy watched the black woman stride away, then looked back at the door. Mark had pushed another coatrack into place and was instructing the custodian to mop up the water on the floor. She sighed. What was she going to do? The mere touch of Mark's fingers had sent her into a tizzy. Had Gerry been right? Hadn't she matured at all from her high-school days?

The band began its first set and Tracy leaned back against the wall, trying to keep her thoughts focused on the students. Idly, she let her eyes wander around the room.

Rose was standing by the refreshment table, talking to Tom Druit, the football coach. Tracy knew she wouldn't stay there long. With all his talk about football, Tom was a bore. So it didn't surprise her a bit when Rose broke away from the coach and came toward her.

"Doesn't he look absolutely scrumptious tonight?" Rose began, glancing across the dance floor.

"Who, Tom?" Tracy knew perfectly well Rose was looking at Mark.

"No, our principal. I've never met a man who made clothes come so alive. It doesn't seem to matter what he wears . . . or doesn't wear." She grinned. "He always looks good, but tonight . . . ummm!"

"Yes, he does look good." Tracy tried to keep her voice even. It was so hard to talk about Mark, especially with Rose.

He looked their way and Rose smiled seductively. Mark smiled back.

"Um-hmm, I think I'll take that man straight home to bed," Rose murmured, then turned to Tracy. "But enough about Mark. How's your love life coming along? Met anyone new?"

"No, there's no one." Tracy swallowed back the lump in her throat and gave a weak excuse. "I haven't had time to date. My Life class has kept me extra busy this year."

That wasn't entirely a lie. She had been busy. But there would have been time for dates, and she'd been asked out, too, but each time she'd said no. It seemed that since meeting Mark, she had no desire to go out with other men.

"You've got to get out and mix!" Rose's pencil-slim eyebrows drew together in a frown. "You can't let one bad experience ruin your life. Look at your mother! She's never hesitated to try again."

"My mother's hardly the one to hold up as an example," scoffed Tracy. "She's the one I *don't* want to emulate. No, I just need a little more time."

She reached over and patted her friend's arm. "But thanks for your concern." It was impossible to dislike Rose—she was so genuinely good-hearted. The fact that Mark found her irresistible shouldn't affect their own friendship.

It wasn't long after Rose walked away that Tracy heard whistles. The band was playing one of its rare slow pieces, and Tracy looked across the dance floor, trying to see what was causing the commotion. Her eyes stopped instantly when she saw Rose and Mark in the middle of the gym, dancing. All the students had stopped to watch them.

Rose seemed molded against Mark—green satin blending into tuxedo black. Her red hair was gathered up in a French twist, but a few hairs strayed sexily down in front of her ears near her long dangling diamond earrings. Above them a mirror ball turned, catching the light and shattering it into thousands of glittering spots. Like Cinderella, Rose seemed to be in the arms of her prince charming.

Tracy turned away and hurried out of the gym. In the girls' bathroom her hand trembled as she pulled out her lipstick and began to touch up her makeup.

Why let the sight of Mark and Rose dancing bother her? Why this knot in the pit of her stomach? So what if she'd felt an electricity between Mark and her earlier— she didn't want him. Didn't want anything to do with such a possessive, domineering man.

But Tracy knew she was caught in the psychological game of sour grapes. For some unfathomable reason, she did want him. Wanted to be the one in his arms. She was jealous of Rose, and she hated the feeling.

The band was playing another fast tune when Tracy returned to the gym. A cup of punch and a few words with the girls serving helped keep her mind occupied, then she strolled back to her position by the wall. Mark was circulating around the room, Rose not far behind, but Tracy forced herself to keep her eyes on the dancers.

She was getting tired of the loud music when the band again played a slow ballad. As the young male lead vocalist began to sing, Tracy felt a tap on her shoulder. "I believe this is our dance, Miss Dexter."

"Mark!" Tracy's heart jumped and her pulse quickened. Then she glanced around the crowded gym. "Oh, but what about Rose?"

"What about Rose?" He smiled, gathering her into his arms. "I danced with her earlier."

Before she could refuse again, they had danced from the sidelines into the throng of students, most of whom, seeing their approach, moved aside. "Sorry, Mr. Prescott," said one boy as he accidentally bumped into them. Then he added, "Miss Dexter, you look beautiful tonight."

"He's right," whispered Mark, drawing her closer. "Beautiful and delectable."

"Mark, don't hold me so tight! What are the kids going to think?" What was Rose going to think, she wondered, and tried to pull free of his grasp. It was impossible.

"Hopefully they're going to be totally confused. Next on my list of dance partners is Miss Webster."

Suddenly Tracy understood his game and laughed. The fifty-year-old woman had reluctantly agreed to help chaperon and had spent most of the evening patrolling the halls, where the music wasn't as loud. "You're going to be known as a playboy," she scolded Mark.

"You'd be surprised how that helps my status with the boys," he grinned. As she relaxed in his arms he added, "That's better. At least now you're not fighting me."

"You could have warned me of your plans," she stated in her defense.

"There wasn't time. Slow tunes are a rarity with this group, and when I dance with a woman I much prefer to have her in my arms. I think it leaves a more lasting impression."

He was right. She would never forget the impression he was having on her. They were dancing so close she felt dwarfed by his size, and her hand looked small and pale where it rested on his shoulder. He wore a cologne that had a subtle musky aroma. She'd smelled it the night he'd held her in his arms in Rose's garden, and now it reminded her of the kisses they'd shared.

"Blue eyes and dimples," he said softly.

Tracy looked up. Mark was gazing down at her, his eyes filled with emotion. "I hope you know," he whispered, "that if I wasn't the principal and this wasn't a school dance, I'd kiss you right here and now."

Pliant in his arms, she knew that if those same conditions weren't true, she'd let him. "You're talking foolishly," she murmured.

"When I hold you in my arms, you make me do foolish things."

They danced slowly to the music, and Tracy felt she'd been lifted to a cloud. Her feet no longer touched the ground. Effortlessly she floated over the gym floor, following each dip and turn Mark made. Their eyes were meshed, silently communicating their pleasure. There was no need for words.

When the song ended, everybody clapped for the band. For a moment longer Mark held her, then he squeezed her hand and let her go. She heard the sound of his own clapping, but her arms were too limp to join in. Even her legs felt rubbery as Mark guided her back to the sidelines.

"Thank you, Miss Dexter." He winked. "Now, if you'll excuse me, I have to make my rounds and check if everybody's behaving."

You're crazy, Tracy told herself as she watched him stroll away. Her heart was spinning and she felt like bursting into song. *A crazy fool.*

It had been a long time since she'd had a man so completely take over her heart. Yet Mark left her confused. While they were dancing, his words and his expression had been loving; yet it all might have been a sham, merely an act for the students. She couldn't be sure.

THE DANCE ENDED at midnight, the bewitching hour. The last song, traditionally, was slow, and Tracy saw Rose start across the room for Mark. When she stopped, Tracy grinned. Mark already had a partner—Miss Webster. The older woman looked a little shocked, then pleased as he took her into his arms.

"I claim the last dance," Bob stated as he came to Tracy's side. "That is, if it's all right with you."

"I'd love to dance with you."

From Bob's arms, moving with the music, Tracy looked around the room. Couples who had been shy when they arrived now chatted freely or gazed adoringly into each other's eyes. Rose had condescended to dance with Tom Druit, although Tracy noticed her eyes were on Mark, not on the coach.

"Going to the faculty Christmas party next week?" asked Bob.

"You know me. I never miss a free meal. How about you and Joanne?"

"We're planning on it. In fact, Joanne's going to use the occasion to tell everybody about the baby."

"Great! I've hated keeping it a secret. I've been so afraid I might accidentally say something."

The dance ended and everybody headed for their coats. Tracy had drawn the cleanup assignment. She would be one of the last to leave. With members of the dance committee, she began to pick up empty paper cups, napkins and pieces of crepe paper. When all that was left were the punch bowl and cookie platters, she sent the teenagers home. In the locker room she washed and dried the glassware, then carried it back into the gym and placed it on a table. Monday morning someone would take the bowl and platters down to the home-economics room.

For a moment she paused and glanced around the large hall. With the students and faculty gone the gym had a barren, lonely look. Only the custodian, his radio blaring, remained to sweep away the memories. Red and white crepe paper was stuffed into garbage cans, the snowflakes taken by students as souvenirs. In the corner the Christmas tree looked small and lonely, its colorful lights no longer glowing. Above her head the mirror ball was motionless, its glitter-making qualities subdued.

"There's something sad about the end of a dance, when everybody's gone," said Mark, his polished black shoes making an echo as he approached her. "What are you doing here so late?"

"I had to clean up, but I think everything's taken care

of now." She swallowed nervously as she gazed into Mark's eyes. The custodian moved into the boys' bathroom, the noise of his radio following him. Mark and she were alone. But raindrops had spotted his tux, and he had a smear of red lipstick on his mouth. Tracy looked away.

"I see it's still raining." It was difficult to keep her voice level.

"Fairly hard."

"I'd better be going." She sidestepped to move around him, but he blocked her way. Tracy tried the other side, and he repeated his actions. Then she looked up. "What are you doing?"

"Keeping you here. There are no students, the dance is over, and I'm sure these old walls don't care if I'm the principal or not."

That he intended to kiss her was evident, but the desire she'd felt earlier was gone. The lipstick smeared on his mouth had killed that. She wouldn't be one of many. "Won't Rose be getting anxious?"

"Why should Rose be anxious?" Putting his hands on her shoulders, he tried to pull her close.

"Isn't she waiting for you, in your car?" Tracy twisted free of his hold and stepped back.

"No."

"I thought you brought her to the dance."

"Nonsense. We simply happened to arrive at the same time." Again Mark moved toward her.

"Sorry, my mistake," she muttered. Part of his plan to keep up appearances, she was certain. No doubt he'd be going to Rose's house as soon as he left the school. Tracy took another step back.

"How long are we going to keep up this cat-and-mouse game?" His eyebrows arched, but he didn't attempt to move closer to her. "Come here."

"What's the matter, wasn't the kiss Rose gave you sufficient?" Tracy snapped. "Can't you wait until later?"

Mark rubbed the back of his hand across his lips, then looked at the red stain on his skin. "I did kiss her, once," he admitted.

"Then that will have to satisfy you until you're in her arms again." Tracy's eyes were bright as she glared at him.

With a lithe movement that took her by surprise, Mark closed the distance between them and grabbed her arm. Jerking her against the hard length of his body, he wrapped his arms around her tightly. "Tracy, stop sounding like a jealous shrew. It's you I want to kiss, not Rose."

"Well, you're not going to," she growled, twisting and pushing. "Maybe you like a lineup, but I'm fussier."

"Stop being childish," he ordered, tightening his grip until she knew there was no escape. "You should know Rose. I walked her to her car, she asked for a good-night kiss and I saw no harm in obliging her."

"I'm sure."

As he lowered his head, his lips coming closer, Tracy turned her face away, pressing her cheek against his jacket. He'd called her childish. That was always Gerry's cop-out. If she'd argued with him, she was being childish, petulant, irrational. . . .

Mark stared down at the top of her head. "You know as well as I do that when we were dancing you wanted me to kiss you. Now, just because I gave Rose a good-night kiss, you refuse?"

"I seem to have a weakness for romantic ballads," she said firmly, not looking up. "All I want now is for you to leave me alone."

Abruptly letting her go, he stepped aside. "As you wish."

Surprised, Tracy stared at him for a second, then hurried for the door, tears filling her eyes. Dammit, she was crying! He was right—earlier she'd wanted that kiss. Her whole body had yearned for it.

Pulling on her raincoat, Tracy ventured out into the night and the rain. It was pouring, and before she reached her car her hair was soaked, with rivulets of water streaming down her face. The pavement was shiny under the parking-lot lights, and puddles were already beginning to form. Then she groaned. Her right rear tire was flat.

A quick look around told her that the custodian and Mark were the only people left at the school besides herself. She wasn't going back inside, however, not after that scene with Mark. She'd never changed a tire, but there was always a first time.

Ignoring the rain and her dress, Tracy unlocked her trunk, then fumbled around until she found all the pieces of the jack. She was trying to pry off the hubcap when she heard Mark say, "Let me do that."

"I can do it," she huffed, tugging on the tire iron until the hubcap sprang off and she stumbled backward, into his waiting arms.

"So you can," he chuckled, setting her back on her feet. "But I think you'd better leave the rest to me." He took the tire iron from her hands. "Have you set the emergency brake?"

"No."

"Do that while I jack up the car."

She obeyed, then stood to the side and watched as the rear of her car jerkily moved higher. "You shouldn't be out here," she remarked, seeing his jacket go limp as the rain soaked into the elegant material. "Your tuxedo's going to be ruined."

"It's a possibility." He began on the lug nuts, dropping each into the hubcap. Tracy doubted if she would have been able to work any of them loose.

"Can I do anything to help?" she asked feebly.

"Keep me company," he grunted as the last lug nut budged and began to turn. "I hope your spare's in good condition."

"I don't know. I've never paid any attention to it. The only time I look in the trunk is when I'm loading and unloading groceries."

"Women!" Mark grumbled, yanking the wheel off the axle. He pulled her spare from the trunk, bounced it, then rolled it into place. "You're in luck. Looks brand-new."

Within minutes he had the spare on and the flat tire in her trunk. She could see that his hands were dirty and she pulled an old beach towel out of her trunk. "I keep this for emergencies."

"Thanks." He wiped his hands, tossed the towel back into the trunk and slammed the lid shut. Then he faced her. "You'd better get that tire fixed right away."

"I will. How can I thank you?" she stammered, afraid to look in his eyes.

"You know how," he said huskily.

"Mark," she pleaded, but he stepped closer and she knew he wasn't going to take no for an answer.

"I don't know why you're fighting the inevitable," he murmured, cupping her chin and lifting her face. "I've stayed away from you for three months, but nothing's changed between us. You want this as much as I do; yet you insist on denying it."

"Because you're not good for me," she moaned. "I can't seem to resist men like you, but it's wrong."

"Why?" He kissed her lightly on her lips, on the tip of her nose, and finally on each of her eyelids.

"You're jealous and possessive and so damned patronizing." She breathed as her hands went up to touch his wet jacket. His red carnation hung limply near her fingertips.

"It seems to me you're the jealous one tonight." His mouth covered hers and he applied several tempting kisses to her lips.

She could feel her resolve melting under his persistence. Her lips were responding, moving with his, and she was the one who invited his tongue into her mouth. His arms slid around her, and he leaned back against her car, pulling her to him. "I do want to possess you," he muttered.

"Oh, Mark," she cried, the rain mixing with the tears that filled her eyes. "Why can't I resist you?"

"Don't try, honey. Don't try." His fingers combed through her wet hair and he kissed her, his tongue probing deep, his lips hungry.

Tracy gasped for breath when he groaned and pressed her head against his chest. She could hear the steady pounding of his heart; lying against the length of him, could feel his growing desire. His hand slipped inside her coat and covered her breast. The night seemed to whirl around them and Tracy dug her fingers into his jacket, afraid she might fly off into the darkness.

"We're getting soaked," he stated, the sound of his laughter rumbling against her ear.

"I don't care." She felt warm in his arms. What did it matter that her hair was soaked and sticking to her cheeks, or that her dress had been ruined? She didn't want to lose the pleasurable sensations of being caressed by this man, who could excite her with a glance. His kisses had vanquished all her doubts. Lifting her head, Tracy gazed up at his face, marveling at the contentment she read in his eyes. Then, rising up on her toes, she touched her lips to his.

"Wouldn't you know it!" he groaned. "Just when you finally decide to stop fighting me, I can't take advantage of the opportunity." Lightly he feathered kisses over her face, his tongue flicking out to taste the raindrops slipping down her cheeks. "Regretfully, I have to drive to Los Angeles tonight."

"Mark?"

"What?" He brushed her wet bangs away from her eyes.

"Did...did you and Rose discuss the possibility of your going to her house tonight?" There, she'd voiced it—asked the question.

"I didn't let the subject even come up."

"Because you have to go to Los Angeles?"

"No, because I didn't want to go." He tilted her chin up so she had to look him squarely in the eyes. "Tracy, there's no need to be jealous of Rose. Now, give me a good-night kiss. I'm sending you home before I change my mind and decide to carry you off into the night."

His kiss was sweet and gentle, and when he let her go and opened her car door, Tracy felt once again as though she were floating on a cloud.

"I'll call you Sunday night," he said. "Sweet dreams."

6

HER DREAMS were anything but sweet, and by morning Tracy wondered what had come over her that she'd so willingly succumbed to Mark's kisses. She hated the jealousy she'd felt toward Rose—hated the envy and resentment. From her experience with Gerry she knew that jealousy was like a cancer—it ate at a person's insides. She'd watched her husband grow more and more suspicious, until finally there was little she could do that didn't make him question her fidelity. His jealousy had stifled her, had killed the love she'd once felt for him. Never would she allow herself to be dominated by such a destructive emotion.

But she didn't know what to do about Mark. Although she'd given in to the attraction she felt, nothing had changed. The problems were still there.

She knew she was merely avoiding the issue, but when Joanne called and invited her to have dinner Sunday night, she quickly accepted. And when she left Bob and Joanne's house at nine-thirty, she didn't drive straight home. Instead she parked near the beach, and for a long time watched the waves break over the sand, their wild, crashing thuds echoing her tumultuous emotions.

The telephone was ringing when she unlocked her

door. To her relief there was no one on the line by the time she reached the kitchen and picked up the receiver. The telephone rang again later while she was taking a bath. It seemed an eternity before the incessant bell was silent.

But the next morning, when Mark called her into his office, there was no way to avoid a confrontation. He was standing behind his desk as she approached. "I tried to get hold of you last night," he said, his eyes boring into hers.

"I was out." She looked through his window, pretending to be interested in the stormy gray sky.

"On a date?" His words were curt as he noticed the way she was avoiding his gaze.

"That's my business." Slowly Tracy looked back. She had to be strong. In his office Mark couldn't kiss and confuse her, but the attraction was still there. It would all be too easy to give in to her desires—and that would be a mistake.

"Have dinner with me tonight."

"No."

With three long strides Mark was around his desk and next to her. "Why, Tracy? Friday night you would have accepted."

"You caught me at a weak moment." She shivered as she looked up into his dark eyes. His jaw was rigid, his mouth firm. Even the pulse at his temple was visible. Tracy knew her words were angering him, but his irritation only fueled her determination.

"Mark, nothing has changed! I don't want to go out with you."

"I don't believe you." He grabbed her arms and jerked her closer.

"Mr. Prescott!" She raised her chin and her body stiffened at his touch. "The door is open. Do you want *everybody* talking about us?"

"Damn!" Releasing his hold, he turned away.

Tracy took a deep breath. "May I leave now?"

"Yes, go," he growled, never looking at her. "And close the door behind you."

Mrs. Baines raised her eyebrows as she passed, and Tracy wondered if the older woman had seen and heard everything. Tracy's legs felt shaky as she walked down the hallway to her room. She'd won a battle, but it was a hollow victory. She'd refused Mark's invitation because she was afraid of where a dinner date might lead. Instead of facing and overcoming the attraction she felt, she'd retreated.

For the next three days Tracy tried to convince herself that she'd done the right thing, that in time she would forget how Mark's kisses had excited her. But Wednesday night, when she arrived at the school gym and saw his Mercedes parked in the lot, she knew it was going to be a long while before she forgot the way she'd melted in his arms. As she walked toward the gym she wondered why he had come.

Early in the fall Rose and she had started a weekly faculty volleyball game. Each Wednesday night they played for two hours, team sizes depending on how many faculty members arrived on that particular night. Bob came sometimes, Sylvia once in a while, but Mark had never attended a game—not even as a spectator.

He was standing next to Rose when Tracy entered the gym. Seeing him dressed in navy blue shorts and a white polo shirt, his legs and arms covered with dark hairs and the taut lines of his muscles etched beneath his tanned skin, she felt more than ever that forgetting him would be impossible. Deny it as she might, she wanted him to take her in his arms again.

"See who I talked into coming to our game." Rose waved Tracy over. "The only problem is he wants to be on your team. I protest!"

"Why are you here tonight?" Tracy asked, trying not to glare too obviously at him. *Are you trying to torture me?* she wanted to ask, but didn't.

"Rose invited me." Mark smiled, ignoring her irritation.

"He's coming to my place afterward...to work." Rose winked at Tracy, then rested her long tapered fingers on Mark's arm. "Why do you insist on playing against me?"

"From the opposite side of the net I can better enjoy your beauty," Mark said with a grin.

Tracy turned away. Quickly she joined the other faculty members who were volleying the ball back and forth over the net.

She could understand why Mark would want to watch Rose. With her flaming red hair she looked absolutely stunning. The scooped neckline of her heather-green top left little to the imagination. Her white shorts were cut high, giving added length to her already long legs and accentuating her narrow hips and firm thighs.

Tracy glanced down at her own outfit. Her red-and-white rugby shirt fit loosely and barely showed the curve of her breasts; her red cotton shorts were the same ones she'd worn in college. Hardly an outfit to turn a man's head. Only her legs did her justice, shapely calves turning to trim ankles above her name-brand tennis shoes.

"Where do you want me to play?" asked Mark, coming up behind her.

"By the net." The farther away the better, she thought. To her dismay the two teams were even in numbers, and there was no way she could argue his decision to play on her side.

"Volley for serve," Rose called. Tracy went to the back row.

Her team won the volley. Tracy would have preferred it the other way. Now she had no choice but to serve first. Normally that wouldn't have been a problem, but Mark's presence was disturbing her more than she liked to admit. Her legs felt rubbery, and her mouth dry. Even before she stepped behind the service line she knew the chances of her playing a decent game were remote.

The first ball she hit glanced off her arm, sliced to the right and plunged through the opening where the net was tied to the poles. "Damn," she muttered, trying not to look at Mark as the ball was returned.

Closing her eyes, she swallowed hard and took in a deep breath. *Get a hold of yourself.* Her face was flushed, her palms sweaty. Nervously she wiped her hands on her shorts, then stepped back behind the line.

Concentrate. She had to stop thinking about Mark, but that was easier said than done. As she focused on the center spot of the opposite court she could see him in her peripheral vision. He flexed his shoulders, his muscles rippling beneath his shirt, and goose bumps ran over her skin.

Although she managed to hit the ball over the net, it

was just about the weakest serve she'd ever executed, and the ball was easily spiked back to an unprepared player at center net. It was Rose's turn to serve and she did it perfectly. Jeff Black missed the return. Point for Rose's side.

Three more times Rose served, and three more times her team made a point. It seemed to Tracy that her own nervousness was catching. She didn't mind losing a game, but this was ridiculous. Trying to forget her anxiety, she yelled encouragement to her teammates. Mark spiked the next ball that came over the net, and this time the other team missed it. Tracy's team rotated one position.

It was then Tracy realized her mistake. A row of teachers had separated them before, but now she found herself positioned next to Mark.

"I see you can't stay away from me," he said with a wink, moving aside only when she reached the net.

"It looks more like you can't stay away from Rose," Tracy returned.

"It was your team I chose to play on." His words were hushed, their verbal sparring barely audible to the other players and certainly not to Rose.

"So you can watch her bend over?"

"Careful, your claws are showing." A ball sailed over the net and he moved to the middle, readying himself for the return.

"I don't like men who play women against each other for their amusement," she hissed when he came back to her side between plays.

"I'm doing no such thing. Rose and I are going to her place to discuss business tonight."

"I'm sure." Another ball whizzed over their heads. It was returned and Mark spiked it for a point.

"Ask her," he continued in a teasing whisper.

"Maybe you two will start with business, but I'm sure it will turn into something else before the night is over."

"Come along and see for yourself." He smiled his challenge, then yelled across the net. "Rose, you don't mind if Tracy comes along tonight, do you? Maybe she'll have some ideas to contribute."

Tracy could read her friend's face and her honest reaction didn't match her words. "Whatever you think, Mark."

"Good. Then it's all settled. We meet at Rose's after the game." He lunged to the side and hit a ball coming toward him.

"I am not going to Rose's tonight!" Tracy muttered, just loud enough for him to hear.

"Why not?"

"Look, I don't want to argue about it. I came to play volleyball...not to get involved in some crazy triangle. Now leave me alone." She tossed her head, her bangs swinging up then dropping just above her eyes.

"By all means." Mark stepped back into position, but his eyes were on her. Angrily Tracy looked away—just as the ball sailed over the net toward her. Jeff Black yelled, but it was too late. The ball hit the floor by her side.

As the game continued, Tracy found herself making more and more mistakes. Normally she was a good player, quick and agile, but twice during the game she nearly ran into Mark as they both went after a ball. Once, trying to avoid him, she fell at his feet; the second time she ran into the net. Her playing was ragged and inconsistent. Not at all like most Wednesday nights.

The game was nearly over, the score tied, when a player on Rose's team hit a high ball. Playing far right in the front row, Tracy saw the chance for a spike. She was poised, her left side to the net, arms back, knees bent like a cat about to pounce. Her weight was resting on the balls of her feet.

The ball arched over the net. It was a high ball—higher than she'd expected. Quickly she adjusted her position. A bit more to the side and farther back. Her right arm raised, she sprang into the air.

It was then she saw Mark. He'd come forward from the center row, planning on spiking the ball as it went over her head. Now his body was also in midair. In unison they were moving in on the white missile. It was too late for either of them to stop.

Their bodies collided with a thud. A strange sound escaped from Tracy as the air was forced from her lungs, then Mark's elbow hit her shoulder, driving her down. As her feet touched the floor her legs gave way, and everything went black.

OUT OF A CONFUSED FOG, Tracy became aware of large powerful hands lifting her. Her cheek brushed against the soft cotton of a damp shirt. As her lungs took in life-giving air, she inhaled the smell of cologne and perspiration. The cologne was familiar—one she liked—and without opening her eyes she knew it was Mark holding her. Sliding her left arm around his solid ribs, she touched his taut back muscles with her fingers. Her right arm hung listlessly at her side.

"Are you all right?" he asked, carrying her to the wooden bleachers.

"I'm not sure." She blinked open her eyes. "What happened?"

"I didn't realize you were still going for that ball until it was too late. Where do you hurt?" Carefully he set her down on the bench.

"My shoulder, I think." Her right side felt numb, but when she tried to move her arm she flinched. "I feel like a freight train ran into me."

Quickly Mark's fingers moved over her shoulder. She could barely feel his touch she was so numb, but when he lifted her arm a sharp pain again shot down her side and she involuntarily cried out.

"Tracy, are you okay?" Rose was leaning close, concern clouding her delicate features.

"I'm fine, just fine," Tracy groaned, shrugging Mark's hands off her shoulder and standing.

Once she was on her feet a new wave of dizziness overcame her, and she wobbled unsteadily. She couldn't pass out again, not in front of everybody. Reaching out, she groped for something to hold on to, then winced as two strong arms wrapped around her.

"I'm taking you to the emergency room," Mark stated, then turned to Rose. "You'll have to finish the game without us."

"But Mark, what about tonight?" asked Rose.

"We'll do it another time." Again he lifted Tracy into his arms. "Where are her coat and purse?"

"Mark, I'm fine, put me down," cried Tracy, twisting weakly to free herself. But the movement brought another swift stab of pain.

"Here they are," one of the other teachers said. "I'll bring them."

"This is ridiculous—I can walk! I was just dizzy but I'm fine now."

"I'm carrying you out to my car, so stop arguing."

"I don't want to go to your car. I don't want to go to the hospital." More and more Tracy was beginning to feel like a helpless child.

"You're going and that's that." At his car he eased her to her feet and, ignoring her angry protests, waited until she was buckled in before walking around to his side. He tossed her purse and coat in the back seat.

"You're treating me like a kid," she grumbled as Mark started the engine. "I'm a grown woman. Don't I have any say in what happens to me?"

"Tracy Dexter, you blacked out once and then nearly fainted a second time. You may have a separated shoulder, or worse. Whether you like it or not, I'm taking care of you!"

"I don't need to be taken care of!" she fumed, sinking back against the seat. It was obvious he wasn't going to listen to her.

They were on the freeway, speeding toward Santa Barbara before she tried again. "Mark, you know if we go to the emergency room it's going to take hours. I blacked out on the court because you knocked the breath out of me. And when I stood up so fast, I simply got a little dizzy. Look." She lifted her arm. "It's better. If it was broken or dislocated, I wouldn't be able to move it like this."

Slowly she rotated her right arm. It was sore, but she knew she was right—no bones had been broken. It seemed for a moment he was going to ignore her, then there was a change in the car's speed and he pulled over to the slower lane of traffic.

"Lift your arm above your head...now forward... to the side," he ordered.

She executed each maneuver.

"Any pain?"

"A little, but it seems to be located where your elbow hit."

"All right, you win," he grumbled, slowing the car even more. "I'll take you home. Which way?"

"Mark, if you'll just drive me back to my car, I can get home by myself."

"Your place or the hospital—which will it be?"

A glance at his determined expression told her the futility of arguing. "Take the next off ramp," she sighed.

Except for a dull ache, her shoulder was almost back to normal by the time he pulled up in front of her house. To be on the safe side, she held her arm close to her body as she slid out of the car and walked to the door. "Thanks for bringing me home," she said, digging into her purse for the house key. "I'll see you tomorrow."

"You'll see me now." Taking the key from her, he opened the door. "After you, Tracy."

"Mark, really...." She shook her head, then stepped inside. Perhaps it would be best to talk now. She wasn't going to spend the rest of the school year torn between desire and disgust.

He paused in the entryway and looked around the modernistic A-frame. The slanted walls were knotty pine, the floor covered with thick plush carpeting in rich orange, gold and brown tones, giving the room a feeling of warmth. Facing the ocean was a wall of glass, divided by narrow wooden bars, creating a Mondrian effect. A long redwood deck, visible outside, was accessible through sliding glass doors.

"Nice," said Mark, stepping farther into the house so that the living room, dining and kitchen areas came into view.

Everything was modern. A counter and bar stools separated the well-equipped kitchen from the glass-topped dining table and cushioned rattan chairs. A free standing, bright orange wood-burning fireplace was flanked by two beige sofas, and there were several over-sized floor pillows stacked by a glass-topped coffee table. A modern Milton Avery painting was hung on the wall that separated the downstairs bedroom and bath from the main living area, while a large mobile of enameled-copper gulls rotated slowly above their heads, suspended from the center rafter. A wooden staircase led to the loft and Tracy's bedroom, its orange, gold and brown railing bars repeating the colors of the rug.

"I like this." Mark walked into the living room and stopped by a glass and white-brick bookcase, where her collection of earthenware pottery was intermingled with sociology and psychology reference books. "But somehow it's not what I expected. You live here by yourself?"

"With Sam." She dropped her purse and coat on one of the couches.

"Sam?" He frowned, his eyes narrowing when he looked up the stairs as if expecting a man to suddenly appear.

Tracy knew what he was thinking. The house was too nice for her salary. Mark figured she was being kept by a man—and that angered her. "Sam's a cat," she retorted.

"A cat?" For a moment he looked at her in disbelief, then laughed. "If only you knew what I was thinking."

"Believe me, I did." She walked over to the sliding glass door and let the gray tiger cat inside. "Not that it's any of your business, but this house belongs to friends of mine. Married friends. John was offered a teaching position at Harvard and loves Boston, but Helen is a native Californian and wants to move back here someday. So while they're debating east versus west, I'm leasing their place."

With a brusque complaining meow Sam marched past both of them toward the kitchen and his food. "Your cat doesn't seem very happy," Mark commented, moving to Tracy's side.

"He's upset with me for putting him out. For a stray I found on the beach, he's quickly adapted to the easy life. A dish of food and a soft couch are the way to his heart."

"And what's the way to your heart?" Mark asked, reaching out to touch her cheek.

"Don't!" Tracy pulled back, determined not to let him confuse her this time.

"Look, I'm sorry I misunderstood about the cat." He moved toward her and she retreated.

"It has nothing to do with Sam." She gestured nervously. "We have to talk."

"I can talk and do other things at the same time." Like a panther he continued to stalk her.

"Maybe you can, but I can't!" Tracy stopped and pointed deliberately toward one of the couches.

"Sit down. Like it or not, you're going to listen to me."

"Is this going to be another lecture on not mixing business with pleasure?" He studied her resolute expression, then walked over to the couch. Once seated, he leaned back. "All right, Miss Dexter, I'm listening."

"I'm not quite sure how to say this." She was surprised he'd given in so easily. "I find you, ah . . . interesting."

"I find you delectable."

"You're not making this easy for me," Tracy protested, disconcerted by the hungry look in his eyes.

"I don't intend to." Mark patted the cushion beside him. "Come sit down. I hate looking up. That's why I became principal, so everybody has to look up to me."

"That's part of the problem. You're the principal. I'm a teacher." Maybe if she did focus on their professional differences, he'd understand.

"It's no problem and you know it. What we do outside of school has no bearing on our working relationship."

"How can you be so sure? What if we had a . . . a relationship, and then it ended? I don't know how I'd react, seeing you every day."

"Tracy, stop worrying that far in the future. We're both adults; we can deal with that situation should it arise. Besides, you don't strike me as the type who falls to pieces, even during an emotional crisis."

He was right, but there were other factors to consider. "What will people say? The other teachers? Parents?"

"That the school board had good taste in hiring you, and that I have equally good taste in wanting to be with you."

"And with Rose?"

"Ah, now we're getting to the root of the problem." He leaned forward, a smile curving his lips. "You're jealous of Rose."

"I am not!" Oh, what a lie. Her quick denial betrayed her almost as much as the tone of her voice. Turning to look outside, she hoped he couldn't see the tremble of her chin. "It's just that Rose and I have been friends ever since I came to Dos Pueblos. I know she likes you and I know you've been dating her. I simply will not hurt her, and I don't think very highly of you for trying to play us against each other."

"That's what you think I've been doing?"

Her shoulders sagged as she looked down at the beach. The waves were ebbing and a pair of lovers were strolling, hand in hand, their footprints visible behind them in the wet sand. With a sigh, she nodded.

"Tracy," Mark murmured close to her ear, and she jumped, startled to discover he'd risen from the couch and come to her side. "I am not dating Rose. I took her out once at the beginning of the year, and we've been working on a project for her Spanish classes, but that's all."

"But the way Rose talks...." Tracy faced him, surprised to discover she wanted to believe him.

"If you're Rose's friend, you know she's a flirt and a dramatist. I enjoy being around her, but she's not my type. I prefer blue-eyed blondes, whose cheeks dimple when they smile."

"Mark..." Tracy weakly protested as he kissed her on the forehead. "What about tonight? You were going to her place."

"To work." Taking her hand, he led her to the couch. "I don't know if Rose has told you or not, but I have a private income, aside from my salary. It's a trust fund my father set up when I was a boy. He did the same for my older brother and for both of my sisters.

"As a result, I am quite well off financially. And rather than give Uncle Sam a big chunk of that money each year, I try to use it in nonprofit, philanthropic endeavors. In other words, I look for tax write-offs. When Rose mentioned that she'd like to find a way to take some of her advanced students on a trip to Spain, I suggested it might be a possibility. We've been working on it ever since."

"That's why you've been spending so much time with her?" Tracy didn't resist when Mark drew her down beside him. "But she said...." Tracy tried to recall exactly what Rose *had* said and realized she had never mentioned anything specific—just that she'd been spending time with Mark. It had been her own jealousy that had blown the situation out of proportion. Exactly what she'd hated in Gerry she'd been guilty of herself. "But last Friday night, at the dance?"

"What about Friday night? You were the one driving me crazy, not Rose."

"If that's so, why did you ask her to dance?" Tracy demanded. "Why did you kiss her?"

"I told you once why I kissed her, and I didn't ask her to dance. She asked me. I had no intentions of dancing with anyone that night, but when she cornered me, I could hardly refuse. After that I decided I'd better be seen dancing with the other single faculty women or rumors would be spreading." He brushed his fingers over her hair, tucking a strand behind her ear. "I wanted to hold you in my arms and was glad for an excuse."

"Oh, Mark," Tracy sighed. There was more—so much more she'd planned on saying. But now she wasn't certain what to think. She'd been wrong about Rose and him. She'd obviously jumped to conclusions. She'd misjudged him...just as Gerry always used to misjudge her. Maybe her picture of Mark had been determined by her former conditioning. Maybe it wasn't fair to classify him with Gerry without knowing him better.

As she gazed into his eyes, Tracy knew it was hopeless. She couldn't fight the attraction any longer.

Sensing her emotional surrender, Mark leaned forward, his arms slipping around her, his mouth covering hers. But as he pulled her close, a sharp pain jabbed her shoulder and she winced.

"That still hurts you?" he asked, drawing back.

"Only when you touched it." She lightly rubbed her fingers over the sore area.

"Take off your shirt."

"What?" She stared at him uncertainly.

"Your shirt. Take it off. Besides the fact that I have two sisters and know what a woman looks like, don't forget I've seen you half dressed before."

When she hesitated he went on, "I promise not to ravish your body. I simply want to check your shoulder." He smiled, and Tracy relaxed. It was concern she read in his eyes, not desire. Carefully she removed her shirt, slowly pulling it over her sore shoulder.

"Now turn around."

She obeyed, tensing as his warm hands touched her

back. He lifted her arm, moving it in various directions and noting her response. Then he began to gently prod the muscle. As he examined her, she absently reached down with her left hand to scratch Sam's head, and the cat rubbed against her leg and purred. But when Mark's fingers pressed against a painfully sensitive spot, Tracy cried out, jerking her hand away from the cat.

"I'm afraid you're going to have a bruise for some time," Mark said. "It's already discolored. Luckily nothing seems to be broken or dislocated."

"I told you as much." She was suddenly aware of her state of undress, of how little her bra concealed.

"I was afraid I'd killed you when you crumpled at my feet," he murmured, leaning forward to kiss the back of her neck.

"Mark?" His name was a plea, and shivers of excitement raced down her spine.

There was a husky tone to his voice when he spoke. "I wasn't going to come to that game tonight, not until Rose mentioned you were the other team captain. Then I knew I couldn't stay away. I wanted to find a way to get you alone...so we could talk...but I never meant to hurt you."

His arms went around her and he pulled her back against his chest. Carefully he protected her bruised shoulder. As she relaxed he kissed her neck, each touch of his lips awakening a new point of pleasure. And when he nipped her shoulder, then soothed the bite with his tongue, Tracy sighed deeply.

She melted against him, against his warm solid chest, and his fingers moved to her breasts. Gently he released the clasp of her bra, replacing the delicate lacy material with his broad, encompassing hands. Slowly he stroked his palms over her nipples, arousing them to firm peaks, and a groan of pleasure escaped from her throat.

"Tracy!" His own voice trembled. He shifted so she faced him, and in his eyes she saw a gleam of lambent passion. "You're so beautiful, so sweet. I want to hold you in my arms, kiss you, make you mine. . . ."

She didn't want to get involved—not with this man. That's what she'd told herself from the very beginning. But she felt the same need, the same yearning to be part of him. When his mouth covered hers, she felt no compulsion to resist—only a deep sense of fulfillment.

It was a hungry kiss, one that went on and on. And as their lips communicated their growing need, their hands relayed similar messages. Her fingers moved through the thick hairs at the back of his head, then splayed out over his back. She wanted to know the feel of him, to memorize every taut muscle, every contour of his spine. And as her hands moved over him his own caressed her breasts, his thumbs rubbed across her nipples, his palms cupped her firm creamy flesh.

When they broke apart, gasping for breath, they gazed at each other, both a little shocked by the fiery passion their explorations had unleashed. "You're so lovely," he moaned, lowering her against the cushions and gazing down at her.

"And you're so . . . so damn good-looking." Reaching up, she combed her fingers through his hair, tousling it so it fell forward across his brow. Suddenly he looked boyish, and she smiled, her cheeks dimpling. "Oh, Mark, you feel so wonderful."

His fingertips traced the contours of her face, his dark

eyes consuming her. Then he lowered his head, reclaiming the sweetness of her mouth. But his kisses didn't stop at her lips. Her cheeks, down the side of her neck—he tasted all of her, nibbling at her velvety skin. And when he reached her breasts, his tongue darted out to encircle an awaiting bud. He drew the nipple into the moist warmth of his mouth, and Tracy dug her fingers into the supple muscles of his back, arching beneath him. Somewhere deep in the center of her a sweet agonized yearning begged to be satisfied.

She closed her eyes and sank back against the cushion. For a while his lips and hands investigated her breasts, then he continued downward, caressing as he went. His hands found their way to the elastic of her waistband, and slowly he lowered her shorts, exposing her bikini panties. His fingers traced a pattern over the filmy nylon, first outlining the triangle of blond hairs, then sliding between her legs to stroke the warmth of her feminine cradle. Flames of passion ignited within her, and Tracy sucked in her breath.

"Honey, I want to know all of you," Mark whispered hoarsely, sensing her readiness. His breathing was shallow, his eyes alight with a need that reflected hers.

"I want to know you, too," she gasped as he lowered his head and kissed the inside of her thighs.

Slowly, deliberately he began to pull down her panties, his fingertips grazing her hips, firing her desire. Then he stood up quickly and reached for his belt.

Neither of them had remembered the cat, not until Mark's tennis shoes had become entangled with the round, furry animal sleeping on the rug. By that time it was too late. With a squall Sam dug in his claws.

Tracy heard Mark gasp, then with a string of ex-pletives, jump away, shaking his leg. Sam was still at-tached to his ankle—a gray ball of fur determined to fend off attack.

Shocked by the quick turn of events, Tracy sat up and stared as with one final shake, Mark dislodged the cat. Sam landed on his feet near the coffee table, gave a dis-gruntled meow and stalked off.

"Damn!" Mark looked down at his leg, at the red scratch above his sock.

It was all too ridiculous, and Tracy started to laugh.

"Fine thing," he glowered. "Your cat nearly kills me, and you think it's funny."

"I'm sorry," she gasped, wiping tears from her eyes as she tried to explain the humor in the situation. "It's. . .it just all seems so ludicrous. There we were, about to. . . to— Then, the next thing I knew Sam was attached to your leg. . .you were hopping around. . . ."

Still laughing, Tracy pulled on her panties and shorts and grabbed her shirt, leaving her bra lying on the couch. She moved to where Mark stood, saying, "I'm sorry, really I am. Sit down, and I'll get something to clean those scratches."

"Does he attack all of your boyfriends?" Mark asked, staring at the cat, who sat across the room glaring back.

"Normally Sam's very friendly and loving."

"Not toward me. That cat doesn't like me." He sat down, shaking his head as he gazed at his scraped skin. "And at the moment I can't say I'm overly fond of him."

"Love me, love my cat," Tracy teased, then wished she'd never said the words. Turning away, she hurried to the bathroom, where she found hydrogen peroxide, cotton balls and a tube of antibacterial ointment.

Love hadn't been mentioned between them. She didn't want it mentioned. Tonight she'd decided not to fight the feelings he aroused—that was all. Many single women enjoyed sex without commitment. She could too.

Sam was still watching Mark when she came back to the couch. "I'm really sorry this happened," she murmured, kneeling in front of him and beginning to bathe the scratches on his leg with peroxide.

As she worked, Mark began combing his long fingers through her hair, gently rubbing her scalp. Only a slight tightening of his touch indicated when she actually hurt him. Carefully she cleaned and medicated the broken skin, knowing some people reacted badly to cat scratches. She hoped Mark wasn't one of them.

At last, finished, she sat beside him, but when Mark reached over to slip his arm around her, Tracy stopped him. "Perhaps what happened was for the best."

"That I doubt."

"What I mean is, we were getting sort of . . . carried away." She raised her hand as he started to protest. "I know I was as much to blame as you, but we didn't think this out."

Mark sighed. "Don't pull back into your shell, Tracy. Don't deny what we just shared."

"I'm not," she said. "But we were going too fast tonight. Look outside. With the lights on like this, anybody out in a boat could have seen us. Here I am, trying to teach teenagers not to get carried away by their emotions, and I almost broke every rule I've given them."

"Such as?" He leaned back and watched her.

"To be prepared; to think of the consequences. Do you realize what we almost did?"

A sensuous smile crossed his lips. "Yes."

Frustrated by his lascivious attitude, Tracy groaned. "Mark, I'm serious. I can't get pregnant. Not in my position."

Reaching over, he drew her close to his side, then kissed her cheek as his fingertips moved lightly up and down her arm. "Let's accept the fact that we're sexually attracted to each other, and that chances are we're going to end up in bed sooner or later. Do you use any contraceptive?"

Tracy shook her head. "Not since my divorce. There hasn't been a need."

"All right then, at least for the time being I'll take care of the matter. There, does that satisfy you?" He nibbled on her earlobe, then teasingly flicked his tongue into her ear, sending a flurry of sensation down her spine.

"It seems like we're moving so fast," she tried to explain. "An hour ago I was determined to put you out of my life forever. Now we're talking about making love. I don't know . . . ."

"I'm a very determined man, Tracy, but I'm also patient. I don't want to rush you. You've been fighting what you felt until now. Let's just take time to get to know each other. Tomorrow night I have to be at a principals' meeting, but Friday is the faculty Christmas party and I've been invited. Will you go with me?"

"Do you think that's a good idea?" Tracy was thinking of the responses of the other teachers—of Rose's reaction.

"I'm not going to hide how I feel about you," he insisted. "For three months I've stayed away—tried to give you time to ease your fears. Now I'm declaring my intentions."

"Which are?"

"Honorable, to be sure." His hand strayed to the front of her shirt and over her unfettered breasts. "Or at least somewhat honorable."

"Mark Prescott, you're incorrigible," she laughed, lifting her face so her lips met his.

Wrapping his arms around her, he squeezed her close, until Tracy gave a sudden gasp. "Damn!" he swore. "Sorry, honey. I forgot about your shoulder again."

"That's all right. I'll survive." She saw the concern in his eyes and, with a trusting sigh, rested her head on his shoulder. "You know, you're a very persuasive man, Mr. Prescott."

"Meaning you'll go with me Friday night?"

"I'll go." She kissed his cheek, then stood. "And now *you'd* better go. I'm going to take a long, hot bath and soak these sore muscles."

"I give an excellent massage," he offered wickedly.

"Beware, or I'll sic my cat on you," she retorted, walking with him to the front door.

"I'll see you in the morning." He kissed her gently, then left.

7

THE NEXT MORNING the sound of the doorbell startled Tracy. She was running late, her stiff shoulder impeding all activities from making breakfast to dressing. A glance at the clock showed it was already seven-fifteen. School would start in an hour, and here she was still in her panties and bra. At the rate she'd been going, it would take her an hour to get dressed.

The doorbell rang again. Grabbing her royal blue velour robe and cursing softly, she hurried down the stairs.

Opening the door a crack, Tracy peeked out, then smiled. "What are you doing here?" she asked, letting the door swing wide.

"Hoping for a cup of coffee." Leaning forward, Mark lightly kissed her lips. "Good morning. How's the shoulder feel?"

"Like it was hit by a freight train...or an overzealous volleyball player." Her cheeks dimpled as she stepped back and let him enter.

"But it's all right?"

"I'm fine," Tracy reassured him. There was no doubt Mark blamed himself for the accident.

"Good," he said with a smile. "So, do I get some coffee?"

"Of course." She pulled her robe closer and led the way to the kitchen. "I'm surprised to see you here. Especially at this hour." Taking a mug from the cupboard, she poured him some coffee.

"I thought you might appreciate a ride this morning, since we left your car at school."

Her car—she'd completely forgotten about it. So many other thoughts had preoccupied her since last night. As she watched Mark lift the mug to his lips, she realized in amazement that ten hours had passed since he'd left her house. It felt in a way as if he'd never left. For hours she'd thought about him, recalling every word and caress they'd shared. Lying on her bed, staring at the ceiling beams, she'd been haunted by his face. And when sleep did come, he'd invaded her dreams.

"I missed you," he said softly, reaching over to touch her cheek, his fingers caressing her skin as if stroking the petal of a rose.

Moving into his arms, Tracy welcomed his kiss. The smell of after-shave and soap lingered on his cheek, and as his tongue slipped into her mouth, she tasted the flavor of coffee. Her hands reached up to his shoulders, her fingers kneading the fine wool of his jacket.

"Hmm, I can't get enough of you," he murmured near her ear. Her robe seemed to part of its own accord, to allow his hands freedom to span her waist, then travel up to her breasts.

"Mark," she said huskily, wondering if she'd lost all self-control. "We have school in less than an hour! I have to get dressed."

"I'd rather see you undressed." As if punctuating his

statement, he unclasped her bra, suddenly baring her small firm breasts. "How tempting to call in sick. Are you certain that shoulder isn't bothering you?"

"Not half as much as you are," Tracy groaned, closing her eyes as his index finger and thumb captured a taut nipple and his lips nuzzled her throat. "Mark, please. You've got to stop this."

"Now that I have you, I never want to let you go."

Tracy's eyes snapped open. "I'm not a possession," she insisted, stepping back out of his reach.

"I didn't mean it that way," Mark protested, surprised by her quick withdrawal.

"I'm enjoying my freedom. An affair is all I want."

His eyebrows rose curiously. "Isn't that usually the man's line?"

"Perhaps at one time, when women were dependent and men were the only ones trying to evade the web of matrimony."

"I don't recall proposing." He was smiling.

"I—" She stopped. No, he hadn't mentioned marriage...or love. So far all they'd spoken about was the urgent physical need they had for each other. She had brought up the subject of love to herself, had fleetingly wondered as she tossed and turned on her bed the night before what it would be like to be married to Mark. She had convinced herself all she wanted was an affair—no strings attached. Now she knew that was all he wanted, too—an affair. There was no reason for her to feel this disappointment.

Taking a deep breath, Tracy finally finished her statement. "I merely wanted to be sure we understood each other. I like honesty in a relationship."

"Oh, we'll have an honest relationship." He grinned, then glanced around the room. "Where's that cat of yours?"

"Sam's outside. How's your leg?"

"Fine. I had excellent nursing last night."

For a moment they stared at each other, and Tracy wondered if he was remembering the moments before he'd tripped on the cat. How close they had come to consummating their desire. How wantonly she'd responded to his caresses. Her cheeks reddened and she looked away. "I'd better get ready."

"Let me," he said, reaching out to catch the loose ends of her bra and bringing them back together.

The gesture was somehow more intimate than before, when he'd unsnapped the clasp. Taken off guard, Tracy stood still, gazing at him as he ran his fingers along the bottom seam, easing the nylon over soft curves until her bra once again fit smoothly and comfortably about her ribs. When he pulled her robe closed and tied the belt around her small waist, she continued looking at him. It wasn't until he said, "I'll finish this coffee while you're dressing," that she moved.

IN HIS CAR they talked about the Christmas assembly, scheduled for that afternoon, and about how hyperactive the students were with vacation only two days away. On the surface they were two educators discussing school events, but there was a constant sexual undercurrent between them—a suggestive glance, a smile, a touch. And when they turned into the parking lot, Mark reached over and gave her hand a squeeze.

"Now we play our roles, Miss Dexter. I doubt if I'll

have time to talk to you today, but I'll call you when I get home."

"Mark?" Her heart seemed lodged in her throat as she faced him. "Do you think of me as...in any way immature?"

His laughter was quick and hearty. "Honey, if I thought that, I could be arrested for what I've been thinking. No, Tracy. You may not look very ancient, but I have no problem telling that you're a mature—and beautiful—woman. In fact, when I've overheard you advising students, I've often thought you sounded far wiser than your years."

"Thank you," she sighed, feeling a warm, happy sensation fill her. "Thank you very much."

As they walked together toward the school building, there was a lightness to her step that belied the soreness in her shoulder. And a smile dimpled her cheeks when she answered a question he asked. She was happy and it showed from the glow of her cheeks to the sapphire blue of her eyes. She tossed back her bangs, the sunlight highlighting their golden color, and laughed when he mentioned that he'd caught a boy sneaking into the girls' locker room. So total was her absorption in the story that Tracy didn't notice Rose pass them in the hallway.

It wasn't until lunch hour, when Rose came into her room, that Tracy realized something was wrong.

"Fine thing when your best friend stabs you in the back," Rose coolly remarked, closing the classroom door after the last student had left the room.

"I don't understand what you mean," said Tracy, looking up from her desk.

"Oh, don't play the innocent. Maybe you can fool others with that baby face of yours, but don't forget, I know you. Or at least I thought I did."

"What are you talking about, Rose? What did I do?" Tracy got up from her chair in alarm. Deep down she did know why Rose was upset. Mark had to be the reason. Maybe he had lied to her. Maybe there really was more between Rose and him than he'd told her.

"You threw yourself at Mark all last night," Rose accused. "I couldn't believe it! You know how much I like him; yet there you were, falling at his feet, asking to come along to my place, then running into him and pretending you were hurt so he'd have to take you home. It was sickening."

"I did not ask to go to your place," Tracy protested. "That was entirely Mark's idea. In fact, I refused to go. And I didn't run into him on purpose. If you'd like this shoulder of mine, you're welcome to it. I can't even lift my arm to write on the board. It's sore to the touch and aches constantly."

"I'm sure that didn't hold you back last night. When I asked Mark what the doctor said about your shoulder, he told me you two never went to the hospital—that he took you straight home." For the first time Rose's eyes were cold. "I didn't realize you were so hard up for a man that you'd steal one from a friend."

"That's not the way it is," Tracy insisted, shocked by the attack.

"Isn't it? Don't take me for a fool, Tracy. You've been after Mark from the very beginning."

"That's not true! I've avoided him."

"Like the night of my party?" Rose smiled at Tracy's

look of surprise. "Oh yes, I saw you two in the garden, kissing."

"You never said anything," gasped Tracy. "I could have explained."

"Explained what? That he forced himself on you?"

About to say yes, Tracy stopped. Mark hadn't truly forced himself on her that night. She could have stopped him. No, it had been her damn curiosity that had put her into that situation. Her curiosity and her attraction. She was as responsible for the consequences as he was.

At her silence, Rose went on. "I should have hated you for what you did, especially considering you knew how I felt about Mark. But no, I tried to be a friend to you. I told him all he wanted to know about you, even stepped aside so you could have him. It wasn't until I realized you two weren't dating that I decided to keep on trying."

Rose shook her head. "What is it with you, anyway? Do you only want him when you think he's interested in me? The night of the Christmas dance I thought I was really getting somewhere with him. But no, you had to ask him to dance. Then you stayed late, so he'd have to leave me and go back inside to see what was wrong—why you hadn't left."

"I didn't ask him to dance; he asked me," Tracy defended. "And I had no choice in the matter of staying late. I'd been assigned to oversee the cleanup. It was my job."

"You have an excuse for everything, don't you? Well, I don't buy it! As far as I'm concerned, you've let me down."

Without another word, Rose turned and left the room. Tracy swallowed back the urge to run after her. After all, there wasn't much she could say. She couldn't explain that none of this had been planned, that if she'd had her way, none of it would have happened. She couldn't possibly explain why she found Mark so damn irresistible.

8

"I'm STARVED," Tracy groaned, her stomach rumbling an affirmation to her statement. "I'd never do well in Europe, where it's fashionable to dine late."

"Sorry we had to miss most of the happy hour, but I had to talk to that boy's father tonight." Mark turned his Mercedes into the parking area of Santa Barbara's world-famous beachfront hotel and found an empty parking spot. "Does the faculty have a Christmas dinner every year?"

"From what I understand, it's been a tradition for over ten years. It was one of the few social functions Holmes ever attended. Sitting at the head table, his wife by his side, he always looked like a king presiding over his subjects. The man loved pomp."

"Well, I'm going to feel like a king with you beside me." Mark turned off the engine and reached across the console to brush his fingertips over her cheek. "You look lovely, Tracy."

There was a glow of passion in his eyes as he leaned toward her, his hand sliding behind her neck to draw her closer. His lips were warm and moist, playing softly across hers, promising so much yet held in check. His free hand rested on her breast, his thumb stroking the silky material of her dress.

It was an intimate caress, and Tracy responded willingly, inviting his tongue into the depth of her mouth. Then with a groan, Mark sat back and released her. "Woman, we'd either better get into that Christmas party now or we're never going to get there."

Without waiting for her response, he opened his door. In the time it took him to come around to her side, Tracy took a quick check in the mirror. There was a blush to her cheeks and her lipstick was smeared a bit. She noted a similar trace of red on Mark's lips when she stood beside him. From her small handbag she pulled a lacy white hankie.

"If you don't want everyone to know what you've been up to, you're going to have to learn to wait until the lipstick has worn off before you kiss us," she teased, wiping his lips, then brushing a trace of lint from his three-piece midnight-blue suit.

"*Us*, as in Rose," he frowned, taking her arm in his and walking with her toward the hotel. "You're not still upset about last Friday, are you?"

"Mark, she really likes you," Tracy tried to explain. "I feel terrible about the way she's acting. She won't even talk to me."

Mark stopped her before they entered the hotel. "I swear I never led Rose on, Tracy," he said sincerely. "Despite what you say she thinks, I never was seriously interested in her. Even if I hadn't met you, I wouldn't be dating her. She's wonderful—lively, beautiful, warm— but she's just not my type. I kissed her good-night last week—casually—because it seemed the thing to do. You asked me to trust you about Bob. Well, now I'm asking you to trust me."

"You didn't do very well about Bob and me," she reminded him. "But I do believe you. It's just that I hate having her upset. She's one of my best friends."

"I'm sorry. If you'd like, I'll talk to her."

"Don't you dare! Rose would be humiliated. I'll just have to give her some time . . . and hope she forgives me as soon as possible."

Tracy shook her head slightly. It still seemed inconceivable that she was about to attend the faculty Christmas party with Mark. For so long she'd convinced herself that he was wrong for her, that he was too much like Gerry. Now those fears seemed groundless. He treated her as a woman, and tonight she even felt like a member of royalty as they entered the elegant hotel.

The Dos Pueblos party was in one of the private banquet rooms, and the festivities were in full swing when Mark and Tracy entered. Tables covered with white linen were graced by lovely china and crystal, and made festive with arrangements of gold ornaments and poinsettias. In one corner there was a Christmas tree decorated in reds and golds, in another a bar, crowded by men and women in dark suits and cocktail dresses.

As Mark took her coat, many eyes turned toward them. Tracy wished it was her rose-colored silk dress with its three-quarter-length dolman sleeves, bateau neckline and gently flared skirt that had caught their attention, but she knew it was Mark's presence by her side that made them curious. Even Bob looked surprised when he glanced up from his drink and saw Mark slip his arm casually around her waist, guiding her toward the bar.

"Over here!" Bob called, after Mark had gotten

drinks for both of them. "Prescott, did Tracy tell you the good news? I'm going to be a father...again," he amended.

"Congratulations!" Mark shook Bob's hand. "Where's your wife? I don't believe I've ever met her."

"Oh, Joanne's somewhere around here." He waved his hand over the crowd of teachers and spouses, then winked at Tracy. "You ought to have heard Rose when she saw Joanne in a maternity dress. She scolded me to no end for not telling her sooner."

"Rose is here?" Tracy hadn't noticed her yet.

"With a regular Adonis. I think they went to the main bar for a dance or two before dinner."

"When *is* dinner? I'm starved." Tracy looked around the room. Except for Rose, it seemed everybody was there.

As if in response, the call to dinner was made. Tracy felt a flush of embarrassment as Mark held her chair for her at the head table. Once again faculty members eyed her, curiosity evident in their questioning expressions.

Sylvia and her husband, Russ, were on Mark's left at the head table, Bob and Joanne next to Tracy. As they all unfolded oversized white linen napkins and placed them on their laps, waitresses moved through the room, quickly setting crab cocktails on each plate. Then the buzz of conversation ceased and no one seemed to care if Tracy was with the principal. At the moment, sweet juicy morsels of shellfish in a tangy red sauce were more interesting than school gossip.

Rose and her escort came back midway through the appetizer course. Tracy looked up and caught their entrance. Wearing a shimmering, low-cut teal silk with a long pencil-slim skirt, her hair piled high on her head, Rose was breathtaking. And the man by her side was equally good-looking, his sun-bleached hair almost white against deeply tanned skin, his blue eyes ethereal, his broad shoulders enhanced by a tailored dinner jacket.

"She doesn't seem to be pining over me," Mark whispered near Tracy's ear.

"Sorry?" quizzed Tracy, searching his face for any signs of regret.

"Not in the least." Reaching over, Mark squeezed her hand.

The crab cocktail was followed by a spinach salad. The food had been paid for from faculty dues, drinks extra. But Mark called in the wine steward, and after a short debate over Chenin Blanc versus Chardonnay, the Chardonnay was ordered, along with a Cabernet Sauvignon. Soon wine was served to everyone who wanted it, and the atmosphere became even more relaxed.

Mark conversed with Sylvia and her husband for a while, as Joanne told Tracy about everyone's reaction to the news of her pregnancy. But when the main course was served—a choice of prime rib or chicken Kiev— Mark turned his attention to Tracy.

As they spoke in intimate, hushed tones, Tracy became oblivious to all else. They were alone in a crowd. She ate, but barely tasted her food. Beneath the table his leg brushed tantalizingly against hers and a warm flush of excitement coursed through her veins. Once his fingers touched her wrist, then glided over the back of her hand. "I wish that everybody wasn't watching us," he whispered near her ear. "In fact, right now I wish we were totally alone."

An ache deep inside her was aroused by the look of undisguised desire in his dark brown eyes. Her pulse raced, a flush of color rising to her cheeks. "Careful, Mr. Prescott," she said a little too breathlessly, "or we'll have tongues wagging more than they already are."

"To proper decorum," he toasted, pursing his lips before they touched the edge of his glass.

With an unsteady hand Tracy lifted her own glass of wine, her gaze locked with his. Almost imperceptibly she returned his airy kiss, then downed the pale liquid. As she turned away, she saw Rose looking at them.

Tracy swore to herself silently. Hurting Rose was the last thing she meant to do; yet it seemed painfully inevitable. Glancing back at Mark, falling deep into the warmth of his gaze, she knew she had lost control over her emotions. Whatever his magic, he'd enchanted her, cast a spell that even logic couldn't exorcise. And tonight, Tracy knew, she would give herself to him willingly if he should ask.

After the waitresses had served dessert and poured coffee, Mark clanked his spoon against the edge of his glass. "Unaccustomed as I am to giving speeches," he began and everybody laughed, "I would like to say a few words tonight."

Standing, he looked over the group. "I can't tell you how much I'm enjoying working with all of you. When I arrived at Dos Pueblos, I wasn't certain what to expect. What I've discovered is a staff motivated by enthusiasm, dedication and a marvelous sense of camaraderie. May the Christmas holidays treat you well, and may the New Year bring us all closer to our goals."

Everyone applauded, then Bob rose to his feet and raised his glass in salute. "To Prescott, who took a ship that was floundering and put it back on course." Then, with a wink at Tracy, he added, "And to his good taste in wine—and women."

Everybody lifted a glass—everyone but Rose, who was looking away. Tracy sighed, wishing she could explain that this wasn't anything she'd planned. She was drawn to Mark, wanted to be with him, and it was useless to pretend otherwise. But she didn't want to hurt Rose.

More toasts were given, then after-dinner drinks were ordered, and people started to move around. When Russ asked Mark a question, Tracy excused herself and worked her way around the tables to the door. There she headed for the restrooms.

After combing her hair, she stood before the mirror in the powder room, redoing her lipstick. In the mirror she saw Rose enter the lounge, and she turned abruptly to face her.

"Well, it seems I owe you an apology for what I said yesterday," Rose stated flatly, coming across the room and opening her handbag to pull out a mother-of-pearl compact. "As much as I hate to admit it, Mark never looked at me the way he's watching you tonight."

"I never tried to take him away from you," Tracy vowed. "I really didn't. Actually I wanted to avoid getting involved with him."

"Why?" There was incredulity in Rose's voice.

"Because Mark reminded me of Gerry." Tracy

shrugged her shoulders, trying to rationalize her behavior. "Or maybe I'm just afraid of making another mistake. Whatever the reason, up until Wednesday night I refused to go out with him." Looking directly at Rose, she tried to make her friend understand. "Really, no matter how it looked, I wasn't trying to take him from you."

Rose shook her head, putting her compact back into her purse. "My pride was hurt, of course. But as long as we're being honest, the truth is you couldn't 'take' Mark from me because I never had him. There was nothing between us, Tracy, much to my regret. Our dates have been nothing more than trips to a tax lawyer, the school board and a travel agency. Wednesday night Mark was coming to my place to work on an itinerary for a trip to Spain for some of my students." She chuckled wryly. "Not that I didn't have other plans for him, which your clumsiness abruptly ended."

"I don't know what was wrong with me that night."

Laughing, Rose patted Tracy's arm. "Watching you tonight, I can tell you what was wrong with you. Maybe you didn't want to get involved with Mark Prescott, but, honey, you do now. Enjoy the man. He's rich, handsome and intelligent. You'll make a perfect pair."

"Then you're not upset anymore?" Tracy studied her hopefully.

"I'm not going to lose a good friend because of a silly misunderstanding. As my mother always says, 'There are other fish in the sea.' What do you think of my catch tonight?"

"He's beautiful." Tracy giggled, then wondered if she'd had a bit too much wine. "Where did you find him?"

"Riding a polo pony—that's about all he does. Austin Wentford the third. He's from old money. More my style, don't you think? And what about Joanne keeping her pregnancy a secret all this time? How long have you known?"

"Since your party in September, but Bob swore me to secrecy. Joanne was afraid she'd miscarry."

"We've got to have a shower for her," Rose announced.

Both of them were laughing when they returned to the banquet room, where some couples were getting their coats and leaving, while others were still deep in conversation. With a "thumbs up" sign, Tracy left Rose with Austin Wentford the third and returned to the main table, where Mark was still talking to Sylvia's husband. Bob and Joanne had left.

"About ready to go?" asked Mark, slipping his arm around her after she sat down.

"Anytime."

"It's been good talking to you, Russ, Sylvia." He nodded to them. "Have a nice Christmas holiday."

THE WINE HAD MADE HER DROWSY, and as they drove to her house, Tracy leaned back in the seat, her eyes half-closed. "You look content," Mark murmured, glancing her way. "Did you have a good time?"

"Marvelous." Thinking back, Tracy chuckled. "Two years ago I went to the Christmas party with Gerry and we got into a terrific row and left before dessert. Last year I went by myself and spent the entire evening talking to Miss Webster about her cats and rosebushes. Did

I have a good time? I had a ball. How about you? Did you enjoy yourself?"

"With you by my side I would have enjoyed a hamburger at a drive-in. Yes, I had a good time. And I meant what I said. It's a good faculty."

"Because you pulled us back together. That was nice of you to buy the wine."

"A gesture of appreciation for all the help I've had. I don't know if I'd compare the faculty to a ship, as Bob did, but it does take everyone working together to make a school run smoothly."

"It took your leadership," Tracy insisted. "Under Holmes, we were splitting up. Teachers either stopped caring or became hostile. I know you don't approve of the way I got that Life class into the schedule, but believe me, going behind Holmes's back was the only way to make any changes."

"I forgave you a long time ago." His hand covered hers and he lifted her fingers to his lips. "Actually, I find it very difficult to disapprove of anything you do."

"Mr. Prescott, are you flirting with me?"

"You bet I am, Miss Dexter. I noticed you and Rose are talking again. All differences settled?"

"We had a good talk." She smiled as she recalled their discussion in the women's restroom.

"I'm glad. You know, some women would have been delighted to take a man away from her; yet it bothered you a lot. 'All's fair in love and war,' the saying goes, but I don't believe that. I admire your integrity."

"Rose has been a real friend to me," Tracy told Mark as he pulled up in front of her house. She waited until he came around to open her door before continuing.

"When I first came to Dos Pueblos, I was a brand-new teacher—wet behind the ears and totally unprepared for the realities of an inept principal and parents who didn't care if 'Johnny' made it or not. Rose took me under her wing, showed me the ropes and helped me learn how to cope with indifference. I owe her so much, I certainly didn't want to repay her by hurting her."

"And now you know you haven't," he stated, his arm sliding around her shoulders as they slowly strolled toward her front door.

"She seems to feel Austin Wentford the third is more her type."

"Probably he is." There was no remorse in Mark's voice. "It amazes me she's a teacher, considering the financial position of her family."

"One could say the same about you," Tracy pointed out, reaching into her purse for the house key.

"I suppose you're right." Taking the key from her hand, Mark unlocked the door.

But he didn't open it, and for a moment they stared at each other, their gazes electrified. Unconsciously Tracy licked her lips, giving them a moist, sensuous look. All through the evening she'd anticipated this moment. Sitting beside Mark at the table, she'd wondered how the night would end. Holding her breath, she waited.

But not for long. Wrapping his arms around her, Mark gathered her close, enfolding her with his solid strength while his mouth gently but firmly claimed hers. Willingly she molded herself to his contours, rising on tiptoes, her lips moving with his. And when the kiss deepened, became all consuming, she welcomed his probing tongue, its invasion into the warm, moist depths of her mouth symbolic of the more intimate form of possession her body yearned to experience.

She was breathless when he raised his head and cradled her close. She could feel the restraint he was exercising, hear the violent thudding of his heart. Her own pulse was no calmer, her legs shaky and weak. In a husky, almost inaudible whisper she asked, "Would you like to come in for a while? I could fix some coffee."

"Tracy," he murmured near her ear, the seductive timbre of his voice stating his desire more clearly than his words. "I want to come in, but not for coffee."

She tilted her face up, to stare into his dark, molten eyes. She understood his unspoken request. The time had come. He had said he would be patient, but they'd both reached the point where holding each other and kissing weren't enough. "Come on in," she whispered.

Opening the door, he followed her into the dark house. Through the window the moon was peeking from behind a cloud. Across the channel they could see the silhouettes of San Miguel and Santa Rosa islands and the outlines of the oil rigs, set past the five-mile offshore drilling limit. Sam saw them enter and jumped down from his perch on the deck railing. His meows could be heard loud and clear through the glass. Tracy snapped on the light and walked across the room to let him in.

"Bringing in your protector?" asked Mark, coming up behind her as she slid open the glass door.

"As long as you stay off his tail, he'll leave you alone."

Resting his hands on her shoulders, Mark pulled Tracy back against him. As he eased off her coat, he

dropped quick, tantalizing kisses along the neckline of
her dress. "I notice you don't have any drapes. How do
people who live in glass houses . . . ?"

"People in glass houses go upstairs, to the bedroom,"
she answered breathlessly.

He looked up at the stairway and nodded. "You never
have given me a complete tour of your house."

He draped her coat over the back of a chair, along
with his jacket and tie. After locking the front door and
turning off the light, Tracy led the way up the stairs.
From the kitchen came the crunching sound of dry cat
food. Sam was content. She wished she could say the
same for herself.

Suddenly a little unsure of herself, Tracy hesitated on
the top landing. She'd slept with only one man in her
life, and he'd taught her everything she knew about sex.
Now she wondered if that was enough. Mark was obviously experienced at lovemaking. Probably did this
often. Staring at her queen-size bed, Tracy felt her
nerves tighten. Would Mark find her lacking as a bed
partner?

Yellows dominated the spacious loft bedroom. Moonlight streaming in from the window facing the ocean
played across her daisy-print quilt. There was no turning back. She'd committed herself . . . wanted this. Slowly she moved across the room.

"The other night you said you hadn't used a contraceptive since your divorce," said Mark, stopping
behind her.

"That's right."

"There hasn't been anyone since your husband?" He
sounded a little incredulous.

Her throat was dry so she licked her lips, then snapped on the globular bedside lamp. "Not since, or before."

"What about last summer? I remember hearing you tell Rose about a man propositioning you."

Surprised he'd recalled that statement she'd made the day they met, Tracy turned to face him. "I didn't even go out with him. Look, maybe this is a mistake. You seem to think I'm experienced at this sort of thing. Well, I'm not."

"The way I feel about you is no mistake." His fingers moved slowly up and down her sleeves, barely grazing the silky material. The slight contact brought tingly goose bumps to her skin and she shivered. "Don't be nervous, honey. I'm glad you haven't been with a lot of men."

"How long...how long has it been for you?" she mustered the courage to ask.

"Since last summer." His thumbs caressed her throat, then he gently tilted her face upward. "Since I met you I haven't been able to get you off my mind."

Months...it had been months since he'd made love to a woman. Her hands touched his shirt sleeves. Perhaps they were just having an affair—two mature adults satisfying a physical need—but it did mean something to him. Words couldn't explain the relief she was experiencing. And when his mouth covered hers, her lips readily responded, growing warm and soft.

"I knew you'd be like this if you ever stopped resisting what you felt," he murmured, gathering her closer. There was no place on her face and neck he didn't cover with kisses.

"You may be disappointed," she confessed, as his palms brushed over her breasts in a delicate caress. "I'm not sure I know how to satisfy a man like you."

"Oh, you'll satisfy me. I have no doubts about that."

"Then I'd better close the curtain."

The light-stealing bamboo curtain pulled easily across the open end of the loft, blocking off their activities from the view of boaters and beach walkers. Kicking off her heels, Tracy reached back for the zipper of her dress.

"Let me do that," Mark suggested.

As her dress slipped from her shoulders to hang loosely around her waist, he nibbled her neck, sending tremors throughout her body. Lightly his fingers slid across her skin, his left hand lingering on her bruise. "How's the shoulder?"

"Tender and a little stiff, but much better."

His hands traveled down her back, pushing her dress free of her hips. In an instant her half-slip followed, lying with her dress in a silk heap around her ankles.

There was something very sensuous about the control he was exercising as he undressed her. Turning her around, he led her closer to the bed. There he paused, his dark gaze assessing her state of dishabille. His thumbs brushed over the silky material of her bra, coming teasingly close to each peak, yet never touching.

Then his restraint ended and he quickly unfastened the catch. Slipping the straps from her shoulders and letting the flimsy bit of material drop to the floor, he gazed at her breasts, now aching for his touch.

"You have beautiful breasts," he said huskily, cupping them in his hands.

"They're not very big."

"They're perfect." Almost reverently he massaged her nipples, bringing them to hard rosy peaks. "Perfect."

Bending his head, he continued his tender adoration, circling each nipple in turn with his lips, then hungrily returned his lips to her mouth, masterfully erasing any lingering self-doubts.

Tracy sucked in her breath when he grasped her bottom and pressed her close, moving his hips suggestively against hers. Flames fanned into a fire. His fingers glided over her body, stroking, caressing, and when he reached the juncture of her thighs, she groaned.

"That's right, Tracy," he rasped, tipping her back onto the quilt and pinning her gently against the mattress. "Want me as much as I want you."

"Oh, Mark, I do," she moaned thickly.

"Are you afraid to touch me?"

"No," she confessed, wondering herself how much longer she could stand it before she tore his clothing off him. Reaching up, she unbuttoned his vest and shirt, then slipped her hands inside to feel the warmth of his skin and the spring of hairs that covered his chest.

"Lower," he groaned, levering himself up on his elbows to give her access. Timid at first, she ran her fingertips over his hips. He was fully aroused. Through his trousers, she could feel his firm outline and knew she wanted nothing between them.

Quickly she loosened his belt, then pulled down his zipper. He helped remove his clothes, letting them fall by the bedside, until he was poised, naked, over her. She arched her hips as he slid her bikini pants down, then closed her eyes as he began to kiss the newly exposed area, his tongue flicking in and out to excite her.

"Oh, what you do to me," she moaned.

"Nothing compared to what you do to me," he rasped, spreading her legs farther apart. "The thoughts I've had these past few months have been immoral."

With infinite patience he caressed her, both his fingers and lips driving her frantic with desire. And when she was certain she couldn't stand it a moment longer, he paused and removed something from his pants pocket. Confused by the delay, Tracy watched him, then realized he was doing as he'd promised—seeing to it she was protected from an unexpected pregnancy.

When at last he was pressed against her, she wrapped her arms around him, arching her hips to meet his thrust. But to her surprise, her body resisted the invasion. He pressed harder, and a small cry of pain escaped from her lips.

"I'm hurting you." He stopped to look down at her passion flushed face.

"It's all right," she gasped. "I'm fine. Really I am." Her need for him was greater than the physical pain he was inflicting.

"I don't want to hurt you, but you feel so good," he groaned, nipping the sensitive lobe of her ear in an attempt to switch her attention from the muscles that were stretching to accommodate his size. She sucked in her breath as another jab of pain confirmed their physical union.

"Relax," Mark coaxed, stilling his hips, his hands resuming their erotic exploration of her body. His expression was troubled. "I never meant to hurt you."

"It's been so long," Tracy tried to explain, melting under his magical touch.

"Then I'll take it easy," Mark promised, his mouth covering hers as he began to move—very slowly, very gently.

It was like her wedding night... yet it wasn't. As her body accepted his, Tracy relaxed and let herself flow with his movements. Knowing where this age-old dance of pleasure would lead them, she was a partner, her own needs matching his.

Intuitively she knew how to please him. But each time she came close to taking him beyond the point of control, he stopped her. "Easy, honey," he soothed, "we have all night."

Lovingly he stroked and praised her, coaxed and caressed, leading her deeper into the world of sensory pleasure. His concern for her pleasure surprised and delighted Tracy. Spiraling higher and higher, she gave herself completely over to her senses.

Time was suspended as they moved together in passion. And when the moment came, she gasped, convulsive waves of pleasure shaking her entire body. Digging her fingers into his arms, crying out his name, she fell into an abyss of ecstasy. The depth of her response shocked her, and Tracy was only vaguely aware that Mark had followed her over that same wonderful pinnacle. Exhausted, panting, she lay by his side, still a part of him, cradled against his hot, damp body.

Slowly they descended, their breathing becoming normal, their bodies cooling. Finally blinking open her eyes, Tracy stared at Mark, not quite certain if she truly understood what had happened between them. "It's never been like that for me," she finally murmured.

"Or for me, either." He kissed her forehead tenderly. "I knew it would be good between us, but I didn't realize it would be that good."

"I thought Gerry and I had a good sex relationship." Her blue eyes glistened as her hand moved to brush a lock of brown hair away from his moist temple. "I never realized...."

"What you were missing?" He chuckled softly. "Neither did I, honey. Neither did I."

Closing her eyes, Tracy marveled at the sense of contentment that had invaded her body. She felt so drowsy, so satisfied, so content. It seemed so right, lying naked on her bed with Mark, her limbs still entwined with his. He smelled male and musky, and she moved her hands over his sides to his hips.

"May I spend the night?" he murmured, feathering kisses over her heavy eyelids.

"Uh-huh." Nestling against him, she dozed off, only to be awakened when Mark moved and began pulling back the quilt.

"You'll feel better if you get under the covers," he explained.

When they'd climbed into bed the sheets seemed cool and crisp against her bare skin. With a flick of a dial, Tracy turned on her electric blanket and in a few seconds was sound asleep.

THE DIGITAL CLOCK on her nightstand said two o'clock when Tracy blinked open her eyes. It was dark in the room, but she was keenly aware of Mark lying next to her. Climbing out of bed, she made her way to the bathroom.

While washing her hands, she gazed into the mirror. Her hair was tousled, her makeup smeared. It was vanity, she knew, but a quick swipe of the brush untangled her hair and an application of cleanser left her face shiny and clean. From her dresser drawer she took a floor-length, yellow nylon gown and slipped it over her head. Quietly she tiptoed back to the bed, carefully easing her body between the sheets.

"I'm awake," Mark said softly, reaching over to touch her side, his fingers moving curiously up, across the smooth material of her nightgown. "Why did you put this on?"

"Modesty, I suppose," she whispered, taking in a breath as he pulled her over to his side of the bed.

"It was a waste of time, you know." Catching a nipple between the silky cloth and his thumb and index finger, he gently massaged the bud until it was firm and erect. "For months I've wanted to be with you like this." In the dark, his mouth found hers.

Immediately she responded to his kiss, then gasped as he began to pull her nightgown up. "Mark, what are you doing?"

"Getting this damn thing out of the way."

In a moment the gown lay on the floor by the bed and his hands moved unrestricted on her breasts. "Now I can get down to the serious business of seducing you."

"I don't believe you!" she laughed, wondering at her own readiness. "I haven't done this since I was first married."

"What happened, anyway?" Mark asked, his hands stilling.

"What do you mean?"

"Why did your marriage break up?"

"Does it matter?" Tracy noted the concern in his tone.

"I don't know. That's why I'm asking."

She supposed it was a reasonable question, and under the circumstances it deserved an answer. "Gerry was forty when he married me—I was nineteen and his third wife. Looking back now, I realize he was my father figure and I was his little girl. The problem is children grow up—a fact he couldn't accept. When I became more independent, his love turned into an irrational jealousy. Finally I couldn't take it any longer."

"Do you still love him?"

"No," she sighed. "It's impossible to keep loving someone who constantly derides you. I don't even know when my love for him died. I wanted so badly for my marriage to work, I clung to the dream long after it ended."

"If you don't still love him, and haven't been involved with anyone else, why then have you been avoiding me for so long?"

Tracy stared into the darkness, barely able to discern his handsome features. "Sometimes you remind me of Gerry," she finally confessed.

"Like when I accused you of having an affair with Bob."

"Yes."

"I'm sorry, honey." Mark drew her into his arms, his breath warm against her ear. "I should have believed you, but you started doing strange things to my logic the moment I laid eyes on you."

"I guess I can't say anything, not after the way I carried on about Rose. Ummm," she purred as he nuzzled her throat with his lips.

"Tell me—" he pushed down the blanket and gently nipped her shoulder "—am I going to have a jealous ex-husband to contend with?"

"Gerry's already remarried. His wife just turned eighteen." Tracy felt sorry for the girl.

"I believe the man has a problem." Mark's hands slid over her breasts, then back up to her face. "And so do I. Tell me, Dr. Dexter, what shall I do? I find I can't keep my hands off one of my staff. I find myself wanting her at all hours of the night."

"I'm not a doctor," Tracy corrected, tweaking the hairs on his chest.

"Ouch! Moot point. Now let me explain the problem." His fingertips traced the contours of her face. "This particular young lady has lovely golden hair, beautiful blue eyes and dimples." He touched her cheeks. "Yes, dimples that turn her smiles into gems."

"And a face that looks like an adolescent's?"

"Nope." Strong but gentle fingers touched her features. "Youthful, but not that youthful." Quickly he added, "I know, don't tell me—you hate looking young."

"I suppose I am overly sensitive about not looking sophisticated."

"Agreed."

"But you don't know what it's like," Tracy groaned, closing her eyes. "It was so damn frustrating, being told by Gerry that I was acting like a kid, and then having other people treat me as if I was one. When I was doing my student teaching I actually had a parent refuse to talk to me because she wouldn't believe I was the teacher."

"She probably hated you for your youthful looks and went out and bought a dozen jars of facial cream." He kissed the tip of her nose and she opened her eyes. She could laugh about it now, but she still hated that woman.

"Stop worrying about it, love. Age will catch up with you sooner or later. And stop comparing me to your ex-husband. I definitely don't see you as anything less than you are."

To emphasize his words, Mark rolled her on top of him, fitting her soft curves against the hard angles of his body. "Let's see if we can repeat what we did earlier."

"Mark...." Her voice trailed off, then turned to a groan as his hands moved downward and his fingertips dipped between her legs. With lightning speed he stirred her to desire once again, and as she flamed in passion, his mouth sought hers. Taking his time, he awoke every nerve ending, until she was certain she would die of pleasure. And, as they drifted slowly back from the heights of their lovemaking, she snuggled against his side.

Life was a series of paths—that was what she told her students. Some people chose the clearly marked, safe routes; others wandered into the unknown. For over a year she'd stuck to a safe, unemotional path, and to-night she'd changed course. Not that she was ready for a long-term commitment....

9

"TRACY."

Her name was uttered in a half whisper, and she almost drifted back into the haze of sleep before she heard Mark's second plea.

"Tracy, wake up. Get this cat off me."

Blinking her eyes, Tracy sat up, trying to separate reality from dreams. Mark lay beside her, covered only by the sheet, and Sam—Sam was positioned between his legs. The cat's front paws were resting on a very sensitive area.

"Sam, what are you—"

"Don't!" rasped Mark as she reached for the cat. "I don't think he likes me, and I'd prefer not to have him digging those claws in when you lift him."

"You're being silly," laughed Tracy. "Why wouldn't Sam like you?"

"Jealousy?"

Tracy was going to laugh again, but seeing the way Sam watched Mark, his green eyes never wavering, she began to wonder. "But I had him neutered."

"No wonder he's jealous! Please, Tracy, just try calling him off."

"Come on, Sam," she called, slipping out of bed and moving toward her closet for a robe. "Good kitty. Want to go outside?"

Mark grunted as the large tiger cat stepped on his crotch, then jumped from the bed to the floor, twitching his tail as he strolled over to rub against Tracy's leg.

"I do believe he considers himself the victor in that confrontation," grumbled Mark, quickly sitting up.

"I'll put him out." Tracy gathered the cat into her arms, suppressing a smile as she heard Sam's contented purr.

"It's a beautiful morning," she declared, returning to the loft. "The sun's out and it's already warm. Who would guess Christmas is less than a week away?"

"Are you always this cheerful in the morning?" Mark reached out to grab her as she neared the bed, and pulled her on top of him.

Tracy squirmed. "Mark, what are you doing?"

"Attacking you."

"I haven't even brushed my teeth." She grimaced. Her mouth tasted like cotton.

"I don't care." Her robe parted and his hands slid under the soft velour to capture her derriere. With a quick twist he'd pinned her against the sheet. His hard outine pressed against her belly.

"Are you always this horny in the morning?" she asked.

"Only when my manhood has been saved by a lovely young damsel."

"I hardly saved your manhood," Tracy laughed, feeling a tingle of excitement between her legs. "I don't know why Sam did that. He rarely even comes up here. The couch is his domain."

"He was protecting your honor."

"I'm afraid he's a bit late for that." She squealed as Mark flipped her onto her back.

Pushing away the sheet, he straddled her, opening her robe so her torso was fully exposed to his view. "God, you're beautiful."

"Mark, it's morning," she began, surprised by the hunger in his eyes. Her words trailed off as his hands began to travel over her body, stroking and caressing every sensitive area he could see. She'd never made love this often.

"What's wrong with making love in the morning?" asked Mark, leaning down to kiss her.

"Nothing." With a luminous smile she melted under his touch.

Although she sensed that his need for her was great, he took his time, his lips and tongue teasing her breasts until each rosy bud had ripened to its fullest. And when his fingertips reached down between her legs, she wrapped her arms around him, pulling his mouth to hers.

Morning merely seemed to intensify the feelings she'd experienced the night before. Call it love or an awakening of her sensuous side, Tracy responded to Mark with a warmth and eagerness she hadn't known before. As soon as he'd taken the precautions he'd promised, she arched her back, inviting him to enter.

Together they found a rhythm that carried them higher and higher in a shared euphoria. When Tracy finally lost control in a frenzy of pleasure she dug her nails into his back, crying out his name. And an instant later he followed, his body bathed in perspiration, his breathing ragged and shallow.

Lying beside him a while later, she studied his languid

features. His eyes were closed and a smile of contentment curved his lips. A dark, rough stubble covered his chin, and she could already feel on her own cheeks a slight sting from his beard. Reaching up, she ran the tip of her finger over the arch of his brow and down the rim of his nose. When her finger outlined his lips, he grabbed it between his teeth, his eyes opening.

Gazing into those velvety depths, Tracy caught her breath. In one night, she realized, she had discovered a lot about being a woman.

"Do you have anything planned for the weekend?" he asked eventually, kissing one of her fingers.

"Nothing, except to buy a Christmas tree. I'm free until Tuesday, when my mother's coming up for the holidays."

"Good. What do you say we take the next few days and get to know each other."

"Sounds great!" Her heart lifted. She'd dreaded the moment he would leave.

"We could spend today sightseeing, then pick up a tree. I really haven't had a chance to see much of Santa Barbara. You could be my guide today." His eyes raked her body and he ran his tongue sensuously over his lips as he added, "Or we could just stay in bed."

"Mark Prescott, you're insatiable." Tracy laughed, sitting up. "I'm going to take a shower."

When she stepped out of the bathroom, her wet hair wrapped in a towel and her robe pulled tightly around her, Mark was gone. But she could hear him moving about below, whistling a cheery tune. The bed had been made, his clothes removed, and the bamboo curtain pulled back. Through the window facing the ocean Tracy could see the water, a shimmering blue.

Quickly she pulled on lacy panties, a pair of designer jeans and a cable-knit pullover. Going to the railing, she looked down. In the kitchen Mark was making coffee. His hair was damp and she realized he must have used the shower in the downstairs bathroom.

He'd put on his pants and shirt, but his sleeves were rolled up and the front of his shirt left unbuttoned, exposing the dark hair on his arms and chest. There was a totally masculine look about him. Barefoot, he moved over to the refrigerator and pulled out a carton of eggs. Then, as if feeling her eyes on him, he glanced up.

"Ready for breakfast?" A smile animated his features, and Tracy basked in the warmth of his gaze.

"Give me five minutes to dry my hair and put on some makeup."

"You've got it."

In the bathroom she hurried to apply some lipstick and blusher, keeping her appearance natural. As she held the blow dryer over the wet stringy strands, her hair lightened in color and fluffed into place.

Mark Prescott, it appeared, was quite domestic.

As she thought about it, Tracy realized she knew very little about Mark. She'd been comparing him to Gerry for so long it was difficult to separate fact from assumption. Mark had been jealous of Bob, but that didn't mean he was neurotic. She herself had been jealous of Rose—and she couldn't really blame Mark for not believing her. Holmes had misled him.

Her silent debate was disturbed by a call from below. "Tracy, your mother's on the phone," Mark yelled.

"I'll be right down."

She ran down the stairs and breathlessly picked up the receiver. "Mom?"

"Tracy Dexter, you scamp! And to think I believed you when all this time you've been telling me you weren't interested in anyone. Is he as good-looking as he sounds?"

"Yes." Tracy smiled, watching Mark move comfortably around the kitchen.

"Did he spend the night?"

"Mother!" Tracy cried, a blush of color rising to her cheeks.

"Honey, you're a twenty-five-year-old divorcée. It certainly isn't going to shock me if you have an affair. Lord knows I'm not the one to cast stones."

"Mom, why did you call?" Tracy asked, hoping her mother would drop the subject. "You are coming for Christmas, aren't you?"

"What's his name?" Obviously she had ignored her question.

"Mark," Tracy said with a sigh. Covering the mouthpiece, she whispered to Mark, "You've aroused my mother's curiosity."

"Trouble?" he asked, cracking an egg into a bowl.

She shook her head.

"What's this Mark do?" her mother persisted.

"He's the principal of Dos Pueblos—my boss. Mom, can we discuss this when you get up here?"

"Just a minute." There was a muffled sound on the other end of the line, then her mother returned. "The reason I called is that I won't be coming to your place for Christmas. Ken and I have decided to get married

Christmas Eve. We'd like you to come down here. Invite this Mark, if you like. Ken says the more the merrier."

"Married?" Tracy groaned, sagging against the counter. "But you said you were through with marriage. Just last summer you admitted you always married the same kind of man. You said yourself that you'd be better off to simply live with Ken."

"I've changed my mind."

"Mom, this will be the fifth time! Ken's a nice guy, but he's just like the others. Don't do it!"

"Tracy Elizabeth Dexter, that's enough," came the stern reply. "It's different with Ken—I know it is. Now if you want to come to my wedding, fine. If not, that's your decision. It's up to you."

Tracy stared at the telephone long after her mother had slammed down the receiver. It wasn't until Mark came to her slide and slipped his arm around her shoulders that she hung up. Somehow the morning had lost its glow.

"Problems?" he asked softly.

"My mother's getting married."

"And you don't approve?"

Tracy shrugged her shoulders. "I met Ken last summer. He's a nice enough man, but he's just like all the others my mom has married. She picks the outdoors type—men who like sports, hunting and fishing. While they're dating and he spends a lot of time with her, that's fine. But after she's married to the man, and he begins to take off to play golf or fish, she starts complaining. She stayed married to my father the longest. I was five when she left him. Since then I've had three stepfathers, all the same type. And it always ends the same way." Tracy bit her lower lip, her blue eyes glistening with tears. "I just can't go. I can't pretend everything's going to be all right."

"Do you think you can talk her out of marrying this guy?"

Tracy shook her head. "Once mom sets her mind to something she's very stubborn. She's in love—or so she thinks. Damn!"

"My youngest sister, Pia, was married last weekend," Mark said, almost as if he was talking to himself. "That's why I had to go down to L.A. I don't like the man, to tell you the truth. As far as I'm concerned he's a limp-wristed playboy. But Pia's my sister. So I went, and I offered my best wishes."

"You're saying I should go? That I should simply ignore what I feel—condone a marriage I know is doomed from the start?" Tracy stared at him. With his support of her mother's position she felt totally isolated.

"No." His eyes caught the quiver of her chin. "I'm simply telling you what *I* had to do. Your decision may be entirely different. When is she getting married?"

"Christmas Eve." It was such short notice. Tears welled in Tracy's eyes, then spilled over and slid down her cheeks. Mark gathered her into his arms, comforting her.

"Don't cry, honey. Please don't cry," he soothed.

But there seemed to be no stopping the tears, and she sobbed until his shirt was wet where her face pressed against the silky material. At last, emotionally drained, she gave a deep sigh. "I just don't know what to do. I'm her only child."

"You have a few days to make up your mind. Would you rather be by yourself?"

"Oh, no!" Solitude was the last thing she wanted. Or perhaps the truth was that she didn't want to be apart from Mark. Forcing a smile, she tried to forget her mother's depressing announcement. "I need an excuse not to think about the wedding."

"Then how about some scrambled eggs and toast?" he suggested, stepping back to study her red-rimmed eyes.

"You're going to spoil me." She wiped away the last of her tears and blew her nose.

"That I think I'd enjoy." Leaning forward, he kissed her forehead. "You set the table while the cook gets to work."

"It always surprises me to see a man in the kitchen," Tracy called over the sound of sizzling butter. "According to all of my stepfathers, cooking is woman's work. And Gerry's attitude wasn't very different."

"I enjoy cooking. When I was married, I used to always fix breakfast. Of course, if I don't cook now I don't eat."

"You were married?" She nearly dropped the plates she'd pulled out of the buffet. She'd never thought of him as being married, and it bothered her that he'd loved another woman enough to ask her to be his wife.

"Not for very long," he answered, pouring the eggs into the hot pan. "It was a mistake from the start. Gail never took my teaching seriously. She thought in time that I'd go into the family business and she could mingle with society. When I finally convinced her that I was never going to follow in my father's footsteps, that I wanted to use my money to start a school for students who have trouble in mainstream education, she left me."

"But how could she?" asked Tracy, bringing the plates to him. How any woman could leave this man was beyond her. Already she felt tied to him by invisible bonds surrounding her heart.

"Very easily. Gail hired a good lawyer, demanded a generous settlement and walked out of my life. Not that I miss her. She was a bitch!"

Vehemently Mark dished the cooked eggs onto the plates, then looked at her shocked expression and laughed. "I'm sorry, Tracy. I still get upset when I think about her."

"It's probably a sign that you still love her," Tracy pointed out ruefully.

"Stop playing psychologist. What I felt for Gail died a long time ago. What I am mad at is myself for being duped. She was a beautiful facade, basically. At least we didn't have much of any depths in common. Here, put these on the table. I'll pour us some coffee."

When they were both seated, buttered toast on a plate in the middle of the table, orange juice and hot coffee by the side, Mark went on. "All Gail ever wanted was my money. Despite the fact that we were married less than six months, she demanded half of everything I owned. And she managed to get a good part of it, too."

"That seems unfair," Tracy declared. She'd asked for very little from Gerry—her clothes, personal belongings and a car.

"Life isn't always fair, but I learned from the experience. Since Gail, I've directed my energies to opening that school. I've always had the money, but not the training. Now I've nearly reached my goal."

"Dos Pueblos is just a stepping stone, isn't it?" Tracy's heart dropped at the sudden thought of him leaving.

"I'll be here for a while." He sat back in the rattan chair, cradling his coffee mug in his hands. "And what do you think of my idea for a special school?"

"That it's a necessity for some students. I read about one in Chicago. They use the tough-love method and a lot of special attention."

"I've studied it, actually. My ideas differ somewhat, but there are many aspects of that school I want to incorporate. Special attention is the key. I want to catch kids before they drop out—show them they're important. I like what you're doing in your Life class, by the way. I hear the kids talking. You've already helped many of them develop a stronger sense of self-esteem. It's great."

"You're going to make me blush, Mr. Prescott," warned Tracy.

"It will only add to your charm."

"I haven't been very charming this morning," she said with a sigh, remembering her mother's call. "I'm sorry I cried on your shoulder. Normally I don't go to pieces like that."

"Your mother's announcement took you by surprise, and I'm always glad to lend a shoulder. And I did find our romp on the bed most charming. . . ."

They worked together clearing the table and washing the dishes. When the counter was clean and the glass tabletop spotless, Tracy slipped on her tennis shoes and Mark finished dressing, leaving off his vest and tie.

"We'll have to stop by my place so I can change and shave, then you're in command," he said as they walked out to his car.

That would be different, Tracy mused. Most men liked to be in charge. When she was first married she hadn't minded the way Gerry organized every outing, as if the task was too great for her. She'd been in awe of him then—the distinguished psychology professor—but in time it had irked her that he refused to follow any of her suggestions. It would be interesting to see how long Mark let her be the guide before he took over.

Mark's apartment was in a modern complex, beautifully landscaped with a kidney-shaped pool in the center patio. Two curvaceous teenagers were already stretched out on beach towels, soaking up the winter sun. Curiously they eyed Tracy as Mark led the way to his front door.

It was difficult to realize that other parts of the country were blanketed by snow and record low temperatures were being reported. Santa Barbara's mild climate attracted tourists year round, and days like this one left no question as to why so many of the rich chose the area for retirement.

Inside, Tracy was surrounded by a conservative decor of blues and greens, and an eclectic combination of modern and traditional furnishings. It was a man's apartment, void of any frilly, feminine touches; yet in its simplicity it mirrored Mark's personality. Here was a man who could afford to be ostentatious, but who found function and quality to be of greater importance. She felt comfortable surrounded by his stereo, his books and his Thomas Eakins paintings.

"Make yourself at home while I get ready," he said, going into the bedroom.

Tracy took him up on his suggestion, getting a glass of water from the kitchen, then browsing through his shelves of books. Many dealt with education, but interspersed among them were mysteries and best-sellers. His tastes in reading material, it appeared, were not unlike hers.

On one wall there was a family photograph. Mark's family, obviously. He was there on the left side of an older couple. His father was distinguished looking—not quite as tall as Mark, his thick hair almost white. His mother, dark haired and regal, seemed strikingly familiar. Then Tracy recognized her—Lucy Lowe, the one-time movie star of the early forties. She was Mark's mother! Suddenly the thought of him being a movie star seemed less remote. That he had chosen to become an educator was even more fantastic than before.

Another man, obviously his older brother, stood on the opposite side of their parents, while seated in front were two beautiful young women, one barely out of her teens, the other pregnant.

"That was taken three years ago," said Mark, looking over her shoulder. "Lana had a baby girl. Her husband was in the service at the time, but he's working for dad, now."

"And this is Pia?" Tracy pointed to the younger girl, marveling at her dark beauty.

"That's Pia. Headstrong and idealistic. I wish I could have talked her out of that marriage. I tried to use my experience as an example, but she refused to see the similarities between Gail and Tony. I give the marriage six months—no longer."

"You never told me your mother was Lucy Lowe." Tracy wanted to get Mark off the subject of ill-fated marriages.

"You never asked. Besides, mom was always just mom to us. She gave up her career when she had Andy."

"Andy's your older brother?"

"Older brother, tormentor and best friend," he said chuckling. "He's married with two kids, loves the business world and has been working with dad since he graduated from college. One day Andrew Prescott Junior will be the head of Prescott Industries."

"And you're not jealous?" She wondered about this beautiful family, wondered if they were really as happy as their smiling faces implied. For most of her life Tracy had dreamed of being a part of a strong nuclear family. Her mother's divorces always destroyed those dreams. Even her own attempt at marriage had failed.

"Jealous of Andy?" Mark sounded surprised. "Never! Dad would have liked me to go into the business, but I didn't want to. So he supported my interest in teaching. I think my parents have been very fair to all of us. They've seen to it we'll never go without. The rest is up to us."

"You're very lucky," she said softly, turning to face him.

If Mark Prescott looked good in a business suit, he looked even better in form-fitting jeans and a navy blue turtleneck sweater. In one hand he held a pair of sunglasses, and as if matching his casual image, a lock of his hair had fallen over his brow.

"What's the matter?" he asked, noticing her expression.

"Nothing. Absolutely nothing." She smiled, reaching up to brush the errant lock back into place. "Except I'm not sure if I'll be able to get you past those two girls outside. You look great."

"Never fear, they consider me the crotchety old principal." His arms wrapped around her, gathering her close. "Besides, I've got what I want. You know I still can't believe you've stopped fighting me."

"I suppose now that the challenge is gone, you'll soon lose interest," Tracy said with a laugh.

"On the contrary, the more I discover about you, the more interesting you become."

She could certainly say the same about him. How long this affair would last, she didn't know, but already she realized there would be a void in her life when it did end. Lifting her head, she sighed as his mouth covered hers in a warm, caring kiss. There was no use worrying about the future. Today was to be a day of fun, a day of discovery.

HER FIRST SUGGESTION was a drive to the harbor, past the Moreton Bay fig tree. Planted over a hundred years before, it had a branch spread so great it could shade ten thousand people at noon.

They parked the Mercedes by the harbor and proceeded on foot along the half-mile breakwater that sheltered the local fishing fleet and hundreds of pleasure craft. And when they tired of watching boats, they moved on to Sterns Wharf.

Delicious aromas wafted from the harbor restaurants,

where seafood specialties were being prepared for luncheon crowds. But it was the smell of fresh fish that greeted their nostrils when they reached the end of the wharf. Young and old alike dangled lines over the side of the pier, while gulls hovered above, squalling and hoping someone would lose his bait or toss them a morsel of food.

Surprised that Mark was so amiably agreeing to her suggestions, Tracy next led him down East Cabrillo Boulevard, to the open-air art show that stretched for almost a mile along the palm-lined sidewalk. Crafts and paintings were displayed by local artists, as they had been every weekend for years.

Mark bought her an earthenware pot for her collection; she bought him a handmade kite. Leaving the pot in his car, they went down to the beach, where they kicked off their shoes and ran along the shoreline, trailing out line until the paper kite soared above the sea, its rag tail a line of orange against a sky of blue.

And when an unexpected change in the wind sent the kite crashing into the water, they held a mock funeral, solemnly burying their toy in a trash can.

Their mourning short-lived, they dodged the small breakers that washed ashore, then picked up broken bits of shells and popped the water-filled polyps of seaweed lying on the sand.

When their hunger took over, they drove to an off-beat Mexican restaurant Tracy loved. Joking about not daring to drink the water, they downed *chilles rellenos* until their mouths burned, and Mexican beer. By then their legs were tired, so Tracy suggested a drive along the foothills—"The Riviera of the West." Once she misdirected him into a little canyon, the road narrow and twisting, but Mark merely laughed and found a way out. Eventually they headed for Mission Santa Barbara.

Beautifully set overlooking the city, the "Queen of the Missions" subdued their mood as they toured its grounds. A guide told them about the early Franciscan monks and the Chumash Indians they'd converted and instructed, taking them back in time. And standing in front of the altar light that had burned constantly since the mission was built, Tracy momentarily remembered her mother and the wedding.

It was late afternoon when they drove away from the Roman-style mission. "What's next, Miss Dexter?" Mark asked, heading the Mercedes down Laguna Street toward town.

"Next?" Tracy groaned. "Sorry, Mr. Prescott, but you're going to have to trade me in for a new tour guide. I'm too tired to even think of buying a Christmas tree."

"You don't get rid of me that easily," he said with a grin. "We can postpone the Christmas tree, but if you're resigning, then it's my turn to make a suggestion. Dinner on the beach. That spot below your house looked perfect for a bonfire and picnic."

"Hot dogs and marshmallows?" She turned to him in surprise. Behind his dark glasses she couldn't see if his eyes were twinkling, but his relaxed smile told her he was enjoying the day as much as she was.

They stopped at a grocery store for hot dogs and buns, along with marshmallows, potato chips, dip, and a bottle of Chianti. Back at her house, Tracy cut an array of fresh vegetables and arranged them in a plastic container. Mark went down to the beach and gathered driftwood for a bonfire. Several trips up and down the zigzagging wooden steps that connected the street level to the beach and they were ready.

Mark had a cheerful fire burning, a stack of wood off to the side. Two long sticks were their cooking utensils, a large plastic cloth their table. As the hot dogs sizzled and bubbled over the flames, the sun began to set. Mark poured some wine into two plastic cups and offered Tracy one.

"To a marvelous day," he toasted, taking a sip. Then, leaning forward, he kissed her. "And to my guide."

"Funny, I didn't really think you'd enjoy some of the things we did today. I mean, in school you're always so proper."

He laughed. "And today I was improper?"

"No, I didn't mean that. It's just...well, I thought you'd consider some of my ideas were rather...immature."

"Like what?"

"Like that kite, and popping the seaweed." Along with getting them lost.

Wrapping his arm around her, Mark pulled her close to his side. "Tracy, I enjoyed everything we did today. I enjoy simply being with you."

"It didn't bother you to do silly things?"

"Not in the least." His lips brushed against her cheek. "That's what I like about you. You're not afraid to try something different. Sure, when I'm at school, I have a certain demeanor I'm expected to maintain, but when it's *my* time, I like to relax and enjoy myself. As we did today."

"Oh, Mark!" Wrapping her arms around his neck, she

pulled his head down to hers. Their lips met, tasting of wine.

Forgotten were the hot dogs as his mouth moved with hers, his tongue sliding over her teeth, then darting past to make contact with her tongue. Wine spilled from their cups as Mark lowered her onto the sand. The sun disappeared into the ocean, momentarily turning the water crimson, but neither Mark nor Tracy noticed. As his hands moved under her sweater, she groaned and he deepened the kiss.

Camouflaged from above by the cliff, they lay entwined on the deserted beach, oblivious to all else but the feel of each other. Tracy had never known such a consuming need to be touched by a man. When he lifted her sweater, she closed her eyes. And as he took her nipple into his warm, moist mouth, a groan escaped from her throat and she ran her fingers over his taut back muscles, massaging and holding him close.

"My gosh, Tracy," he gasped, pushing himself away and looking down at her. "If I don't stop now, I'm going to make love to you right here and now. And considering this isn't a private beach, that might be a little risky."

Flushed, her breathing ragged, Tracy watched in surprise as Mark rose to his feet and walked down to the shoreline and straight into the water. As the waves broke around his ankles, soaking his jeans, he stared out at the ocean, hands on his hips, his back to her.

Rolling up her pant legs, Tracy followed him, and standing by his side, she let the cool water and the steady rhythm of the sea soothe her turbulent emotions. Neither of them spoke for a long while, then Mark took her hand and leaned over to kiss her forehead.

"This is my favorite time of the day," he said, pausing to listen to the high-pitched call of a sandpiper. "Everything seems so peaceful."

"In the early 1800s this area might not have been quite so peaceful," Tracy said, looking out across the calm water. "All along this area of the coast there were smugglers' coves, where brash *contrabandistas*, American otter traders, would rendezvous with the Chumash Indians to exchange clothing, hardware and costume jewelry for pelts. The Spaniards had forbidden such commerce, but under the cover of darkness trade went on. Right where we're now standing the Chumash might have once waited for the signal to take their crudely made driftwood boats out to the smugglers."

"You make the area come alive, Tracy." Mark scanned the horizon with his eyes as if looking for ancient mariners.

But there were none. The sky grew darker and the stars began to sparkle above them. At last Mark squeezed her hand. "Think you can hold off attacking my body until after we eat?"

"Attacking your body?" she cried as they walked back to the bonfire. "I didn't attack your body."

"Ah, but you did, my love." He feigned a submissive attitude and sighed. "And let's face it, I'm putty in your hands."

"Mark Prescott, you make me sound like the aggressor," she railed, hooting with laughter. "I guess I did start things tonight."

"Which pleased me so much." The warmth in his voice verified his words. Then he laughed in turn.

"While the lovers are away, the cat will play...or in this case, eat."

Sam sat on the edge of the plastic tablecloth, devouring raw hot dogs from the package.

"Why didn't he eat one of these?" cried Tracy, lifting up the sticks—two shriveled, charred masses that had once been hot dogs.

"Face it, Tracy, that cat of yours has good taste. He adopted you, didn't he? Hey, that's all you get, Sam," Mark insisted, pushing the cat away from the package.

With a glower from his green eyes and a flick of his tail, Sam strolled over to Tracy, curling up by her side and beginning to purr.

"Why do I always feel I've lost the battle to him?" asked Mark, eyeing the cat. He offered Sam the burnt hot dogs, but the cat refused to be tempted.

They roasted the remaining unmolested hot dogs, munched on chips and raw vegetables, and drank the wine. And when it came to marshmallows, they argued over which was better, lightly tanned ones or charred with a liquidy center. Mark groaned when she intentionally burned hers to a crisp, and she laughed when his perfectly browned one caught fire.

Afterward, they lay back on the sand, the fire crackling beside them. "Ever been on a grunion hunt?" asked Tracy.

"Come on, I know they don't run until March. What are you trying to pull on me now? And no, I don't want to go snipe hunting, either."

"You're too suspicious," she laughed, rolling over on one side to gaze at his profile. "I just wondered if you'd ever been grunion fishing?"

"Once when I was in my teens. A bunch of us drove up to one of the beaches the paper had reported as a possible site for a run. I remember we built a bonfire and told ghost stories. Lying under a full moon, I thought for a while that that was all it was going to be—a beach party—then someone yelled, and it looked like an aberration was taking place. The waves had turned silver! Great schools of little fish rushed into the shallows and onto the beach. It was amazing—the females writhing into the sand, depositing their eggs, the males circling them, releasing their milt. We ran down and caught as many as we could with our hands." He smiled and looked at her, the firelight reflecting in his dark eyes. "It was fun. Why?"

"I've never been."

"Never? How long have you lived here?"

"Since I transferred to the university. I met Gerry that spring and was too much in love to care about grunion spawning. After we were married, I discovered Gerry thought such things were pretty foolish. . . . Anyway, he wasn't interested. After I left him, I thought I would try it, but so far I haven't."

"Then we'll go this year, and we'll catch a mess and have a fish fry. How's that sound?"

Sam answered with a meow, and they both laughed, Mark reaching over to roughly rub the cat behind his ears. "I think the way to this boy's heart is through his stomach. Let's go for a walk."

Mark and Tracy strolled along the beach, walking hand in hand. Tracy felt light-headed from the wine, exhausted from the day. Breathing in the crisp salty air, she tried to clear the cobwebs from her mind.

"Tired?" asked Mark, stopping to face her.

"A little." The moonlight illuminated her golden hair until it shone like a halo around her face.

"May I spend the night with you?" he asked, a slight catch in his voice telling her the depth of emotion he was experiencing as he gazed down into her eyes.

"I'd like that," she hoarsely responded.

Returning to the bonfire, Mark doused the coals and buried them with sand. Tracy gathered what was left of the food. The beach cleared of all litter, they carried their belongings up the steps.

10

"WHERE TO TODAY?" Mark asked, his arm hugging her close to his body.

It had been late before they'd drifted off into a deep, languorous sleep, and her mind was still hazy as her lids fluttered but didn't open.

Her drugged senses reminded her of their hours of love-making. He smelled male and musky, and she nuzzled her face closer to the warmth of his chest. A hair-roughened leg draped across her smooth thigh, then moved slowly up and down in a stroking motion. "Heaven!" Tracy murmured, feeling happy and contented.

"Hmm, I think that may be a bit too far."

"Huh?" Her eyes blinked and she looked up, trying to figure out what he was talking about.

"Heaven, that is. I was thinking of somewhere more local." He grinned down at her. "Ready to be my sight-seeing guide again?"

"What time is it?" she groaned, eyeing the light filtering through the bamboo curtain.

"Nearly ten."

"Ten!" Tracy twisted free of his arms and legs and sat up. She combed her fingers through her tousled blond locks, brushing her bangs back into place. "I never sleep this late."

"Never say never," he laughed, pushing back the sheet and getting out of bed. "By the way, I put Sam out. He came upstairs about an hour ago, complaining. I think he's getting used to me."

Tracy wondered if Mark had gone downstairs as he now appeared. Wearing no clothes, he was the epitome of manhood. Gerry had always worn pajamas. . . .

Darn, why was she always comparing the two of them? Her eyes raked over Mark's well-proportioned athletic body. She'd seen him working out with some of the boys after school. He put time into keeping his body in shape and it showed.

"Let's take a shower while you decide on today's agenda," suggested Mark, bending over to kiss her before gathering her up in his arms.

She expected him to put her down in the bathroom, then leave. But when he closed the door and turned on the shower, Tracy realized he was staying.

It seemed silly to be embarrassed. They'd shared so much the nights before. He knew every inch of her body, just as she knew his. Yet as he stepped into the spray of hot water, Tracy hesitated.

"What's the matter?" he asked, holding the shower door open.

"I've never taken a shower with a man."

"Great! A first!" Before she could react, a wet hand came out and grabbed her wrist, pulling her under the water.

"Sometimes you surprise me," he chuckled as their bodies were pelted by the fine spray. "In so many ways you're mature beyond your years. Yet at times you show a childlike innocence."

"I am not a child!" Tracy's blue eyes flashed with sudden anger. "Just because I'm...I'm modest doesn't make me immature."

"I didn't say that," Mark corrected. "In no way are you immature. But you do have an air of innocence about you, which I find delightful."

"Gerry saw me as a child," she went on, too disturbed to recognize the difference in meaning. "He...."

"I am not Gerry!"

The force of Mark's words caused Tracy to take in a breath. Curiously she noted how dark his eyes seemed, droplets of water dangling like jewels on sable lashes. She had just told herself the same thing. Perhaps she was being overly sensitive. "I know that," she finally said, reaching out with her fingertip to follow a trail of water through the wavy brown hairs on his chest.

"You're a woman. A very beautiful woman," he sighed, leaning forward to kiss her. "And I want you with me—here, in bed, everywhere."

"And here is where I want to be."

A smile replaced his frown and he picked up the bar of soap and began to make a lather. His hands glided over her body as he soaped her, and as the water rinsed her clean, his lips and tongue followed his hands, first nuzzling her neck, then moving down to her breasts, which he cupped in his palms. Unable to constrain herself, Tracy groaned in pleasure and reached out to hold him.

His hair was wet and thick, and she twisted a strand between her fingers, her breathing quickening. There was a child in everyone—that's what her psychology books had said. The unrestrained, impulsive side of a person, which had to be controlled by the adult. Or call it id versus ego, the labels psychologists used. As Mark's lips worked their way down over her belly, his tongue dipping into her navel, she knew the primitive, impulsive side of her was gaining control. All modesty forgotten, it was pure physical pleasure she longed to experience.

"Ohhhh," she groaned as his fingers found the core of her femininity.

Her body burned with desire as his lips blazed a trail along her inner thigh. He nipped her soft skin, then soothed the love bite with his lips. As he spread her legs apart, she leaned on him, closing her eyes, hardly hearing the constant patter of water striking the tub. His tongue and hands were working magic, caressing, probing, arousing. "Ohhh, Mark, I can't take much more," she gasped.

Immediately the intimate exploration ended, leaving her with a longing ache that begged to be satisfied. Opening her eyes, she watched him stand, then felt his hands cup her bottom, his fingers pressed into her soft, pliant flesh. Pulled against him, touching his male hardness, she knew his arousal was as great as hers.

"I take it you've never made love in a shower, either," he murmured, capturing her earlobe between his lips.

"No," she groaned as he slowly rotated his hips, pressing her closer.

"I should have brought something in with me. I'll have to go back to the bedroom."

"It's all right, I'm safe," she cried, stopping him before he moved away.

"You're sure?" He studied her, the shower spraying over both of them.

"I'm sure. I figured it out the other night."

Suddenly he lifted her, and wrapping his arms around her thighs, brought her hips up against his taut flat belly. With a single movement, he fitted himself to her form.

The position was unstable, at best—in a wet shower, precarious. He wobbled, stepped back and regained his footing. Clinging to him, her arms wrapped around his neck, Tracy gazed into his eyes, waiting to see what would come next. Twice he began a slow, rhythmic movement with his hips, only to stop and readjust his balance.

"It looked easy enough in the book," he groaned, his arms locking more tightly around her thighs as he once again tried to pick up a rhythm.

"You read sex books?" she giggled, hanging on to him, afraid of falling. The mood had been lost.

"I confiscated it from one of the boys. *A Hundred and One Positions.*"

"And this is one of them?" She gasped, digging her nails into his shoulders as he nearly slipped.

"Yes," he grunted. "Oh, damn! Forget it!" He set her back on her feet, exasperation and frustration showing on his face. "I must be getting old."

"You're not old." But her amusement had turned to curiosity. "Come with me," she urged, turning off the water and opening the shower door. The bathroom was steamy and warm, but she shivered, partially in anticipation. "Lie down."

He looked suspiciously at the large yellow throw rug beside the shower, then back at her.

"Lie down, on your back," she repeated. "Now close your eyes."

Bending over him, Tracy began to touch and caress his body in much the same way he had hers. As her hands massaged his shoulders, spanned his ribs and rubbed across his flat belly, her lips trailed a line of kisses down his throat to his male nipples. He sucked in his breath, his eyes momentarily opening as her tongue encircled one small peak.

Lightly her fingers slid over his hips, then along the inside of his thighs. For a moment she examined the cat scratches on his leg, the ragged lines healing nicely, then her fingers boldly traveled higher, to investigate the innate differences in their anatomies. A feeling of exhilaration filled her as she lifted her head to look into his warm, glowing eyes. She was now the one in control of their pleasure, and it was exciting.

Feathering butterfly kisses along the same path her hand had traversed, Tracy continued her sensuous exploration. As his muscles involuntarily twitched and tensed, she knew she was bringing him to the same fevered pitch she had known only a short while before.

"Tracy," he gasped, "do you have any idea how good this feels?"

"Do you want me to go on?" she asked, her tongue darting out to further incite him.

"Yes . . . oh, God, yes."

She straddled him, leaning forward, using her body to tease him. Her breasts brushed across his chest, his springy hairs tickling her nipples. "Which position is this one in the book?" she asked, rubbing her hips against his, touching his hardness.

"Who cares?" he groaned, then sighed as she completed the union of their bodies.

Arms rigid, eyes closed, she rode him, letting her movements flow naturally. They were on a journey—a race. Faster and faster she moved, picking up the pace. His fingers raked over her bottom, dug into her soft inner thighs, and she cried out. He arched his hips, and she rode on.

Breathing ragged, she gasped for breath. *Oh, how she needed him. . . needed his strength, his determination.*

Perspiration covered her body. The room was hot and muggy, making her light-headed. For a moment she faltered. He picked up the rhythm, driving her on, urging her with wild, erotic words. *He needed her, too.*

Then came the rush, the surge. He crossed that invisible line first, saying her name, calling her his love. Or did she just think he had? Her fingers dug into his arms as her body convulsed. Then she collapsed onto his chest.

The thud of his heart was like the beat of hooves. She listened, gasping for air, her own pulse pounding in her ears. Slowly the tension left their bodies, arms relaxed their holds, and heartbeats returned to normal. Mark's lips found hers, and his kiss told his satisfaction as clearly as his sigh.

"I've never done that before," she confessed, shivering as her body cooled.

"You can practice on me any time you like." He smiled, entranced by her sparkling blue eyes. "I get the feeling you really liked having me under your control."

Tracy rolled off his chest and sat beside him, surprised herself by her heady sense of accomplishment. "I think it's a symbolic victory," she analyzed. "For four years I was the classical helpless female—dominated in so many ways. I never would have dared do that with Gerry. He wouldn't have let me."

"So you had to see if I would?"

She considered that, then shook her head. "It was the other way around. With you I felt I could. You're not afraid of your masculinity."

"And Gerry was?" Mark sat up beside her, and she nodded.

"Not that Gerry was gay, or even bisexual. He simply felt...inadequate, on so many levels. I think he questioned his virility. As a result, he was afraid to show any emotion, afraid it might make him appear weak. The one time I ever saw him cry was when I left him. I thought it was a breakthrough, that he might actually change, become more sensitive to my needs. But during our separation I realized he wouldn't. He always had to put me down. . . ."

Mark cradled her face in his hands. "Tracy, he was a fool. You're a wonderful person—fun and enthusiastic and talented. You're a beautiful, intelligent woman, and it's his loss for not appreciating the fact. Now, let's take that shower and decide how to spend the afternoon."

A drive to Solvang was their choice. A few clouds dotted the sky, forerunners of a Pacific storm. But the day was warm, and Tracy pulled on a blue-and-white, horizontally striped sailor's top, white chinos and blue deck shoes.

After their shower and breakfast, Mark left to change clothes. He returned looking debonair and handsome. Brown cords, suede Hush Puppies and a tan cashmere sweater over a gold cotton shirt gave him a casual air. His dark glasses added a touch of mystery.

They took the scenic route to Solvang. Up through the San Marcos Pass, north along the rim of the Santa Ynez Range, and past Lake Cachuma, Santa Barbara's man-made reservoir. And when she'd exhausted her limited knowledge of the area's history, Tracy leaned back in the seat and watched Mark drive. He reached over to squeeze her hand, and they rode the remaining distance in a comfortable silence.

Solvang was only forty-five minutes from Santa Barbara, but its Scandinavian architecture, windmills and cobblestone walks treated visitors to a taste of Denmark. "Sunny Valley" was the translation of its name. Established in the early 1900s beside Mission Santa Ines, its initial purpose had been to educate immigrants from Denmark. But the little village had been quickly discovered by tourists as a cultural enclave and a great place to buy European goods and food.

The afternoon was everything Tracy had hoped for: an escape from the problems of her mother's upcoming wedding, a time to get to know Mark. They toured the mission's museum, church and cemetery, then drank hot coffee and ate sweet Danish pastries, fresh from the bakery. In the souvenir shops Mark purchased a pair of *traeskos*—wooden shoes—for his niece, and a pan for making *aebleskive* pancakes for his older sister. Tracy found a catnip ball for Sam and a hand-embroidered apron for her mother. And when they tired of shopping, they drove to Buellton, Home of the Split-Pea Soup, and had dinner—including split-pea soup.

It was dark when Mark parked in front of the A-frame and walked Tracy to her door. For a moment they stood outside, awkwardly staring at each other.

"Would you like to come in?" Tracy finally asked.

"For coffee?" His lips curved upward as he leaned forward and lightly brushed a kiss across her forehead.

"If you like."

"You know what I'd like, but I don't want to overstay my welcome. I don't want you to tire of me."

Grinning, she unlocked the door and led the way inside.

The next morning, even before she opened her eyes, Tracy was acutely aware of Mark's absence. She missed the warm solid feel of his body beside her, the sound of his deep, even breathing. How quickly she'd gotten used to having him around. The pillow was crushed where his head had once lain, only the scent of his cologne remaining. The now-familiar aroma aroused a longing in her.

Sitting up, Tracy stared across the room at the bamboo curtain and strained her ears. But there were no sounds below, no bustling about in the kitchen, no familiar whistling—no sounds at all, except for those of the house itself.

Getting out of bed, she stepped over the nightgown lying crumpled on the floor. She'd come to bed decently covered, but that hadn't lasted long. Mark had wanted nothing between them, and the gown had been quickly removed. As she recalled their lovemaking, a satisfied smile stole across her face. Then she shivered in the cold and quickly walked over to the closet to find her warm velour robe.

It was chilly downstairs, the sky an ominous gray. Choppy, windblown waves were breaking on the beach, frothy whitecaps highlighting the water's turbulence. The storm was getting closer.

Propped by the telephone, she found a note.

Morning, Sleepyhead. Sam's out. Thought I'd give you a few hours to yourself. I shall return—with lunch and a surprise..

Mark's signature was scrawled beneath the message and Tracy smiled. The emptiness she'd felt since waking was replaced by a warm glow. He would be back . . . and soon. Gazing around the room, she ran her fingers through her rumpled hair. The house needed to be cleaned, but a hot bath and a shampoo would be first on her agenda.

Luxuriating in the steamy tub, Tracy lay back and closed her eyes. It had been a wonderful weekend. Never had she felt more relaxed. Being with Mark was like coming alive, discovering the other half of herself. He was a steadying force, yet not rigid. Suddenly Tracy couldn't imagine a day without Mark, a day without the sound of his voice. Maybe she was falling in love with him. . . .

Nonsense! she chastised herself, her eyes snapping open. She shouldn't even consider such a notion.

She'd thought she loved Gerry, but it had been blind adoration combined with physical attraction. Undoubtedly that was what she was experiencing with Mark. He was a good-looking man, a good lover and interesting to be around. But love? Love meant commitment, marriage, taking a chance and possibly failing. No, an affair was all she wanted . . . all Mark had said he wanted. She picked up the bar of soap and began to lather herself. Her mother's wedding was what she had to think about, not romantic hogwash.

When she was dressed in designer jeans and a soft turquoise angora sweater, her hair brushed into place and her makeup carefully applied, Tracy tackled the necessary chores. Time flew by as she vacuumed, dusted, made the bed and washed her breakfast dishes. Knowing Mark would be back for lunch gave impetus to her cleaning. She was sitting at the counter enjoying a hot cup of tea, everything done, when the doorbell rang.

"Ho, ho, ho. And a Mer...ry Christmas!" Mark greeted, shaking out a small, well-shaped Douglas fir, its needles densely packed, branches evenly spaced.

"You bought a Christmas tree!" she exclaimed in delight, stepping back as he moved past her and into the house.

"Where do you want it?" He paused near the fireplace and looked around the room.

Immediately Tracy pointed to a spot near the sliding glass door. "There, where I had last year's. It can be seen from the channel and won't be in the way."

Set before the window, the tree was dwarfed by the house's massive triangular lines. Instructing Mark to bring an end table out of the spare bedroom, Tracy placed the small tree on top, giving it added height.

"Maybe I should have bought a bigger tree," said Mark, stepping back to observe the total effect.

"It's perfect," Tracy assured him, moving to his side and rising on her tiptoes to kiss his cheek. "Wait until you see it with lights and ornaments. Thank you so much for buying it."

"My pleasure," he murmured, wrapping his arms around her and giving her a proper kiss. "Miss me?"

She had—more than she liked to admit—but she

wasn't about to tell him. "Miss you?" she mockingly pouted. "Just like a man. The moment there's housework to be done you skip out."

He glanced around the room and nodded his approval. "Looks like my timing was perfect. Ready for lunch?"

"Aren't I always? The way I've been eating, I'll soon weigh a ton."

Mark's hands spanned her small waist and he shook his head. "You're just right. Besides, I know a book that shows how to burn off those calories."

"What book is that?"

He answered with a lecherous grin. "*A Hundred and One Positions*, by...."

"You're a dirty old man, Prescott. What would the school board say if they knew?" she laughed.

"We'll keep it a secret."

Sam came up from the beach and rubbed against the sliding glass door, his gray fur ruffled by the wind. Still laughing, Tracy pulled out of Mark's arms and walked over to let the cat inside.

"What's he do, just show up for meals?"

"And a cozy bed. Usually he stays out all day. It must be getting bad out there."

"Before I get rained on, or he takes another bite out of my leg, I'd better go get lunch."

Sam arched his back suspiciously when he first saw the Christmas tree. Cautiously he approached, circled the table, then jumped up for a closer look. Finally satisfied that the tree was both inanimate and inedible, he gave a disdainful sniff, hopped down and strolled out to the kitchen and his feed dish.

"Originally I'd thought we might have a picnic on the beach," Mark huffed, carrying in two sacks of groceries and pushing the door closed behind him. "But the wind's blowing so hard, I'm afraid all we'd be eating would be sand. The tree almost blew off the car twice on the way over here."

Setting the bags on the counter, he began to pull out packages of cheese, meats, marinated mushrooms and artichoke hearts, olives and finally a loaf of sourdough French bread and a jug of red wine.

"What did you do, raid a delicatessen?"

"Just about. Leaning down, he gave Sam a slice of prosciutto.

"I hope you know you're spoiling my cat," she scolded.

"It's called a peace offering. Hopefully he won't attack the hand that feeds him . . . or, in my case, the leg of the man who feeds him."

Tracy set the table while Mark sliced the bread and arranged the food on a platter. The aromatic smell of pine was already filling the house. "It's a beautiful tree," she said, pausing to study its nearly perfect shape. "And I appreciate your buying it, but really you shouldn't have. What if I decide to go to San Diego? To my mother's wedding?"

"Then you enjoy it for a day or two, or however long you're here."

"Maybe you should take it to your apartment."

"No," he said solemnly, bringing the platter of food to the table. "If you go to San Diego, I'll go down to Los Angeles—to my folks. You still haven't decided about your mother's wedding?"

"No." She sighed, sitting down as he poured the wine. "Deep down I know I should go."

"I'm beginning to wish you wouldn't. I don't want these days to end."

Afraid to look into his eyes, Tracy gazed at the ruby-red wine in her glass. Those same feelings were also holding back her final decision. She too was enjoying being with him. Perhaps enjoying it too much.

"Tracy?"

His voice was husky, filled with emotion, and she looked up. But whatever Mark had been about to say remained unspoken. Instead the somber look on his face suddenly brightened, and he smiled and lifted his glass in a toast. "To us."

"To us," she returned.

They ate and talked, and after the meal was finished and the kitchen cleaned, Tracy brought out her box of Christmas decorations. Tchaikovsky's *Nutcracker Suite* on the stereo provided the proper holiday background music. Humming the familiar strains, she handed Mark the lights to string, then started hanging her brightly painted handcrafted ornaments.

The rain began before they finished, the wind pelting enormous drops against the glass. The sky was growing darker by the hour, the temperature dropping. And when the last bit of tinsel had been strung from the tree's laden branches, Mark built a fire in the fireplace.

For the rest of the afternoon they sat at the dining table, playing cards and talking. It was the sort of homey atmosphere Tracy loved. Even Sam was enjoying himself. Fascinated by the blinking lights of the tree, the cat jumped up on the end table and began to bat at the limbs, jerking his paw back when it struck a warm bulb, and becoming more curious when a ceramic gingerbread man fell to the floor. Twice Tracy had to leave her cards to pick up a fallen ornament and put him back down on the rug.

At last, tiring of the game, Sam gave up and settled himself in front of the fire.

Tracy pulled two steaks out of the freezer, and when it was dark, they put away their cards and started dinner. "Here I am, thinking about food again," she laughed as Mark broiled the steaks and she prepared a large salad.

"Don't worry, you'll get plenty of exercise . . . later."

"Who said anything about you staying later?" she teasingly returned.

"Would you send a man out into a storm like this?"

As if on cue, the wind howled ominously.

"You win," she laughed, carrying the salad, wine and French bread to the coffee table.

They sat on the living-room rug in front of the fireplace and ate. And when she was done, Tracy leaned back on a floor pillow and sipped her wine. The only light in the room was the glow of the fire and the twinkling lights of the tree. Outside it was pitch-dark, the patter of rain against the windowpanes a constant reminder of the storm.

"I could almost become an advocate of Christmas on a night like this," sighed Tracy.

"You don't like Christmas?" asked Mark, sneaking Sam a bite of steak.

"Oh, I like the religious aspects, but I can't say it's one of my favorite holidays. Besides the commercialism, it always seems to be the most trying season for me." She leaned on one elbow and watched Mark stroke her cat. "You know, the highest rate of suicide occurs at this time of year."

"You're not considering suicide, are you?" He frowned, giving her his undivided attention.

"Of course not," she laughed, "unless it's by eating myself to death. No, what I mean is, everybody thinks of Christmas as a family time, a happy time, but it's not that way for everyone."

"What has it been like for you?" he asked, moving over and stretching out beside her.

"Lonely." She swirled the remaining wine around in her glass and watched the glow of the fire through its ruby depths. "There's not much family when you're an only child, and so is your mother. One of mom's husbands—I think it was her second—had several children from another marriage. That Christmas was a wild one. Kids all over the place. I loved it. But she divorced him the next year."

"If you want family, you should come with me Christmas Day," Mark offered quietly. "It's never lonely at the Prescott house. Besides my two sisters and my brother, there are now husbands, wives, nieces, nephews, aunts, uncles and cousins. Dinner is always a hectic, noisy, totally enjoyable event."

She envied him. "Sounds like fun. I thought it would be like that for me when I married Gerry, but I later discovered he didn't especially like his family . . . didn't enjoy holidays much either. Our first Christmas I did invite all of his children over for the afternoon. What a fiasco."

"What happened?"

"They argued, they bickered, they whined, and the youngest one cried the entire time. Gerry was no help. Half an hour after the girls arrived—he had four daughters from his previous marriages—he holed up in his study. Having them over was my idea, he said, not his. So for three hours I tried to entertain four kids who would have far rather been home with their mothers, playing with their new toys. It was ridiculous. Needless to say, I never suggested that again."

"How is it you and Gerry never had any children?" Mark asked, reaching over to rub the back of her neck in a soothing, sensuous manner.

"Gerry didn't want any more children. He said they were too demanding, that he wanted me all to himself."

"And what about you? Didn't you want children?"

Tracy sighed, putting her glass on the coffee table and snuggling close to him. "When were first married, all I could think about was having a baby—Gerry's baby. Naively I thought he would change his mind. But he didn't. Later I realized it was for the best. He was so jealous, so possessive—he just didn't know how to share, not even with his own kids. I'm sure that was part of the reason for his first two divorces."

"And what about now? Do you still want babies?"

She laughed and turned to face him. "We've come a long way, Mr. Prescott, but I don't think the school board's ready for pregnant unwed teachers yet."

"What if you were married?"

Solemnly she shook her head. "I'm not sure if I'll ever remarry. Growing up, I watched my mother jump from one marriage to the next. I vowed I would be different, that I would be married once and only once. Well, my judgment in picking a husband wasn't any better than my mother's. Here I am, twenty-five and already a divorcée. But I'm not going to be like her in all ways. Once is enough."

"So now you advocate having affairs, not getting involved?" he muttered.

Tracy lowered her eyes, disturbed by the condemnation in his tone. "It's not like I'm being promiscuous," she defended. "You're my first affair since my divorce."

"Your first," he growled. "And just how many more do you plan on having?"

"I don't know." Tracy sat up and looked down at him. "What difference does it make?"

He also sat up, facing her. "The difference is, I don't want to share you . . . not now and not in the future. Dammit, Tracy, I'm in love with you."

"No!" she cried.

"Yes! You know these past three days have been special. Hell, they've been fabulous. We're good for each other."

"You can't love me," she moaned, shaking her head.

"But I do. Tracy Dexter, I love you." Pushing her back down onto the floor pillow, Mark pressed her to the rug. Skillfully he captured her lips, silencing any further protests.

The storm outside was nothing compared to the turmoil raging inside of her. It couldn't be love he felt. Sexual desire, attraction, need . . . but not love! She struggled not to respond, but felt herself weakening. He was drawing her into a whirling vortex of emotion. Denial became anger, then frustration. What of her own feelings? What about the longing she'd sensed that morning when he was gone? The emptiness? Was hers more than a physical need? Each breath-stealing kiss left her more confused.

"Oh, Mark," she groaned. "Why?"

"Because you're the one woman for me," he hoarsely whispered near her ear. "I want to be with you, day and night, for the rest of my life."

"It's too soon," she protested softly.

"It's been far too long." His kiss reiterated his desire.

Incredibly, willingly, she surrendered to him, knowing only an overpowering need that he alone could satisfy. Kisses turned to caresses. Her clothes were removed, then his. Aroused beyond control, she was caught in a whirlwind of passion, a rampage of sensuality. Expertly his hands traveled over her body, awakening a flurry of sensations, and she responded with wild, tempestuous abandon.

"I love you," he cried as their bodies melded, his pleasure becoming hers.

Clinging to his shoulders, with waves of ecstasy pulsing through her, Tracy wanted to repeat his words, but couldn't. And when they lay exhausted in each other's arms, tears began to slip down her cheeks. Turning away, she stared at the blurred image of the Christmas tree for a long time.

"I hope you were right about being safe," he said at last, his fingertips moving lazily over her damp back. "I'm afraid that time *I* forgot."

"I'm safe," she murmured, blinking back more tears.

"Tracy, why are you so afraid to accept my love? Trust me. I know this is right."

"I wish I could be that sure," she groaned. "Maybe I just need some time. Maybe being away from you for a few days will help

"Don't go," he begged, turning her to face him. "Stay with me. Spend Christmas with my family. Let me share the joy of a large family. Let me show you how much my parents love each other after thirty-eight years of marriage. Let me show you it *can* work."

"I can't, really I can't. It has nothing to do with us," Tracy tried to explain. "It's like you with your sister. Whether I approve or not, I have to go to the wedding. She's my mother."

"And when you come back? What then?" Tenderly he wiped away her tears.

"I don't know." As she gazed into his dark eyes, so black in the dimly lit room, she knew what it felt like to love. But try as she might, the words wouldn't come. Stifled by crippling memories, she said nothing.

WHEN TRACY RETURNED to Santa Barbara, she still didn't know what to do about Mark. She'd missed him far more than she liked to admit. And when he answered her call, her heartbeat raced and her palms turned sweaty. But seeing her mother's blind adoration of Ken had made Tracy even more wary.

Mark came over right away, the fact that he was still in sweat shirt and jeans as much a proof of his eagerness as the short time it took him to drive from his apartment to her house. "How'd it go?" he asked when he finally released her from his embrace, the feel of his lips still on hers.

"About as I expected," she said, leading him into the living room where she had a cheerful fire burning. "Mom's in love. Ken's perfect. Peace on earth, goodwill to all. Et cetera, et cetera."

"You sound cynical." He sat beside her, his arm sliding along the back of the couch, his fingers playing with a lock of her golden hair.

"I don't see how this marriage is going to succeed any more than any of the others did. Mom hasn't changed. She wants a man at home, constantly idolizing her. Ken loves her...or at least he acts like he does. But he also loves to play golf, go to baseball games, fish—the usual. And she hates doing any of those things."

"Doesn't she understand him yet? You said they've been living together." Mark leaned closer and dropped adoring little kisses along her cheek.

"Up to now Ken's been spending most of his time with mom. My mother's a very beautiful woman and looks young for her age. Men have a tendency to try and sweep her off her feet."

"Like mother, like daughter." He kissed her throat, his tongue darting out to measure the increase in her pulse.

"Mark, I can't concentrate when you do that," she groaned. And she did need to concentrate. She needed to know if he was right—if she was like her mother. She pulled away. "Are you sure it's not just my body you want?"

"At the moment it does seem to have a certain appeal." His hand moved over her beige sweater, his palm rubbing across her breast.

"Well, I'm not a sex object, one you can jealously possess," Tracy snapped, jerking away and standing.

Mark stared up at her. "I've never thought of you that way!"

"Haven't you?" she questioned, thinking back over all their encounters. "From the very first you've wanted your hands on me. You were dating Rose, yet you tried to seduce me in her garden. You were jealous of Bob because you wanted me for yourself."

"Maybe I did feel some jealousy toward Bob," Mark admitted. "But it was the fact that he was married, that you were—or I thought you were—breaking up his marriage, that upset me most. And I wasn't dating Rose! That was something you erroneously assumed."

"How would you react if I went out with another man?"

"Is that what you want to do?" He eyed her coolly from the couch. "Did you meet someone while you were in San Diego?"

"No, of course not," she returned. "But someday you'll see me with another man. What then? Will you go into a jealous rage?"

Mark stood to face her. "It would depend on what you were doing with him. If the two of you were in bed, you can bet I'd be upset. If you were just talking, I'd probably join the conversation. Tracy, stop trying to compare me to Gerry!"

"Why, because I'll see the similarities? You're so handsome, Mark—and so in control all the time. I couldn't see Gerry for what he really was because I idolized him. Well, maybe I'm idolizing you, too."

"I'm not perfect!"

"No, you're not," she pointed out. "We've already established that you're the jealous type—just like Gerry."

"Tracy, I love you! Besides, look at yourself. You were jealous of Rose."

"And I hated it."

"Honey, you're a psychology major. You know jealousy is the result of a poor self-image, or a rivalry of some sort. I hate to sound conceited, but a lack of confidence is not one of my weaknesses. And I don't think it's one of yours, either. I believe you love me, and you know how I feel about you. Now stop worrying."

"That's another thing," she fumed. "Just like Gerry, you want to order me around, play the dictator."

"That's not true! I'm almost always cooperative. Don't forget that other morning in the bathroom," he reminded her. "I was pretty submissive that day, I would say."

"Were you? Or were you simply playing with me?"

"I am tired of being compared to your monstrous ex-husband!" he growled, his expression as dark as his eyes. "Yes, there are times I'm dictatorial. I have to be, in my position. Perhaps I do tend to give too many orders. But I haven't noticed you cowering at my feet. And let me point out that you're acting rather childishly right now. You're making something out of nothing. This entire argument is adolescent!"

"Just as I thought!" cried Tracy, carried away by her temper. "Maybe you're attracted to me sexually, but you don't respect me as a woman. You never have and you never will."

"If sex was all I was after, I never would have told you I loved you!"

"Words!" Her sapphire eyes were sparking, her chin held high. "Words mean nothing, words that will be taken back as soon as I'm your 'possession.' Let me tell you, Mark Prescott, I'm not in love with you. I will never again allow myself to be dominated and demeaned by a man. Not by you, not by Gerry—not by any man. I am not going to repeat my mistake. Not like my mother has."

"That's it, isn't it—all of this is because of your mother's wedding. You're upset with your mom, and you're taking it out on me." Mark stepped toward her and reached for her shoulders.

Tracy quickly dodged his grasp, putting the couch between them. "Mom's wedding simply made things clearer. You're the one who started all this, telling me you loved me. I was willing to have an affair with you, but no, you had to go and ruin everything. Mark, it just won't work between us."

"Why?" His eyes narrowed menacingly. "Because you have some silly idea that I'm like your ex-husband? What do I have to say or do to make you believe I do respect you, that you're wrong? Dammit, Tracy, come here before I—"

"Sure, threaten me!" Tracy cried, moving out of his reach when he came around the couch. "That's what Gerry always used to do. Once he even hit me. Is that what you'll do, Mark?"

He glowered at her for a moment, and Tracy realized she'd gone too far. Then he sighed, his shoulders sagging. Slowly he shook his head. "No, I'd never hit you. Tracy, why are you so determined to end this?"

"Because there's no future for us." She looked down at the rug, tears forming in her eyes. "Not now."

"Then why did you call me tonight? Ask me over here?" His voice was tightly controlled.

"It was a mistake. I'm sorry. I thought . . . ." Tears slid down her cheeks. "I don't know what I thought. I only know what must be."

"And what must be?" he asked.

"I can't see you anymore."

"That's going to be a bit impossible, considering school resumes in less than a week." His tone was sarcastic.

"You know what I mean," she hoarsely responded, avoiding his eyes.

"And what if you're pregnant? There were those two times...."

"I'm not," she nearly whispered.

"You're sure?"

Looking up, she met his piercing stare. "I'm sure."

"Give us a chance, Tracy," he pleaded. "Maybe I did rush you. Maybe you're not ready for a commitment. But can't we go on seeing each other?"

Shaking her head, she willed herself to be strong. He watched her, knowing all too well how determined she could be. At last he sighed and his shoulders slumped further.

"All right, Tracy, have it your way. But remember, I do love you. And not just for your body. I love you, and I think you love me. I'm a patient man. I've waited this long to find a woman like you; I can wait a little longer. But someday you're going to have to stop lumping all men into the same category with your ex-husband. When you do, I hope I'm still around."

He waited for a response, but she made none. Without another word, he turned and walked away. Tracy heard the front door open, then close. The room was silent, except for the crackling of the fire. Sam came up and rubbed against her leg. Tracy looked down, but the tiger cat was no more than a blur through her tears.

SHE WASN'T SURE how it would be, working with Mark when school resumed. And what would she say to Rose? Bob? To all of the teachers who had seen her with Mark at the Christmas party?

Actually it was easier than she expected.

Perhaps it was her pale, drawn look, or the weight

she lost after her return from San Diego. Rose asked very little, accepting almost too readily her statement that Mark and she had found they had nothing in common. Bob merely nodded and changed the subject. Finally Mark was the only one she had to face.

Tracy was surprised when he sent a note to her classroom, asking her to come to his office during her conference period. With leaden feet she walked down the hallway, then waited for Mrs. Baines to knock on his closed door.

"You can go in," the older woman said, returning to her desk.

"Close the door behind you," Mark ordered as Tracy entered his office.

"Mark, we've said all there is to say," she began, doing as he said.

"This is not a personal matter. Sit down."

If he loved her, it certainly didn't show in his eyes. Dark and cold, he watched her cross the room and sit rigidly in front of his desk. There was no sign of warmth in his expression, and she wondered if it had all been a dream. Could this be the same man who had held her lovingly in his arms? Whose lips had ignited a fire within her? "Then why did you want to see me?" she asked.

"The superintendent has decided to set up a board of principals and teachers to revamp the district curriculum. For the next few months we will be meeting once a week to establish goals and decide how best to accomplish those goals. You will be the teacher representing this school."

"Me?" She sat in stunned silence. "I'm not even a

tenure teacher. I've only been here two years. Certainly there are others at Dos Pueblos who are more qualified."

"The choice has been made, and it's you."

"Mark," she said, standing, "making me go to these meetings with you isn't going to change how I feel."

His eyes skimmed over her drawn features and thin body, and for an instant his gaze softened, then the shield returned. "As I said before, this is not a personal matter. You've been chosen because you have an excellent rapport with the students, you're a very good teacher, and your Life class is innovative. The superintendent wants to incorporate a similar class district wide. You're the best one I know to inform this board of your experiences."

"When will the meetings be held?" she asked, hoping some conflict in schedule would give her an excuse to refuse.

"After school Thursdays. I checked, and you're free then."

He had her coming and going. There was no way to say no. Tracy stared at him, wondering how he could be so unemotional. He must not realize how just being in the room with him was tearing her to pieces. Logically she knew it was wrong to want him, but the attraction was there. Maybe it would always be there.

He noticed when she sighed. "Does that mean you'll participate?"

"It seems you've given me no alternative. When's the first meeting?"

"Thursday. We'll take my car."

"I'd rather drive myself."

"We'll take my car," he repeated, a cold cynical smile curving his lips. "I'm the dictator, remember. Like Gerry." Then he looked down at the papers on his desk. "Now, if you don't mind, I have a lot of work to do. As I'm sure you also have."

There was nothing to do but leave. Walking back to her room, Tracy tried to recall exactly what Mark had said and how he'd looked. Their meeting hadn't gone at all as she'd expected. He hadn't mentioned missing her or wanting her to change her mind. In fact, he seemed to have completely dismissed their brief affair. To her dismay, tears welled in her eyes. It seemed as if all she did lately was cry. She'd made the right decision—she was sure she had—but she felt miserable.

ALL DAY THURSDAY Tracy dreaded that final bell. And when it did come, she jumped. Mark had told her to meet him at his office as soon as possible after school. Quickly she answered questions, cleared the students from her room, picked up her purse and headed for the main office.

He was waiting for her. Without a word, he led the way to his car. Nothing was said until he pulled out of the school's parking lot, then he glanced her way. "You look terrible. You're pale, haggard, and you've lost too much weight."

"I seem to have picked up a virus," she said, lamely excusing her appearance.

"I'm sure," was his gruff reply. "You haven't changed your mind about us?"

"No." The word was hoarsely whispered, and Tracy stared out the side window, struggling not to lose control of her emotions. She had to be firm. She would never forgive herself if she gave in now. She wouldn't be like her mother. She wouldn't make the same mistake twice.

"So be it." It was a harsh response, and for the remainder of the drive into Santa Barbara, neither of them spoke.

Tracy was thankful the meeting began only minutes after they arrived. It gave her something to focus on besides her misery. The superintendent introduced all of the people in the room, then began an explanation of what he hoped to accomplish in the weeks to come. And as the hour slowly passed, Tracy forced herself to think about educational objectives and forget her ambivalent emotions.

On the drive back to Dos Pueblos and her car, Mark asked her opinion of ideas that had been suggested, their conversation revolving strictly around possible curriculum changes.

That became the pattern over the next three months. They attended the meetings together, riding there and back in Mark's car, discussing the proposed ideas. When she began looking forward to their weekly get-togethers, Tracy wasn't sure. No more than she could pinpoint when they first started staying in town for dinner.

Over the meal they would talk about the changes that should be made in the curriculum. But more and more often their conversations would diverge, covering politics, religion and other common interests. Not always did they agree, but never did Tracy feel patronized or put down. She was a woman stating her opinion—an opinion Mark didn't always share, but at least respected.

It was usually late and dark before Mark dropped her off at her car. He would follow her home, honking his horn and driving away when she snapped on her front light and waved goodbye. Not once did he ask to come in or make reference to that one weekend they had shared. And not once did he ask her out. If his leg accidentally brushed against hers, or his hand touched her body, he apologized. He was always the proper gentleman—until Tracy wanted to scream out her frustration.

Slowly, over the weeks, she'd realized Mark was nothing like Gerry—never had been. Any similarities were strictly superficial. Her paranoia of repeating a mistake had blinded her to the truth. She did love him, loved him more than she thought possible. But by the time Tracy had recognized this fact, Mark's patience had obviously run out.

Peggy Nichols was one of the teachers on the curriculum council. Dark haired, vivacious and very pretty, she often came over to talk to Mark before or after the meetings. At first Tracy hadn't thought anything of the relationship. Mark talked to a lot of people, both men and women, asking advice, listening and making comments. But the night Peggy invited herself along to dinner, Tracy realized she had more than an academic interest in Mark. And his willing acceptance of the suggestion appeared to confirm Tracy's worst fears. She'd waited too long. Mark Prescott was now interested in another woman.

During the meal Tracy couldn't help but watch. There were the smiles, the heady laughter at each other's jokes, the personal questions. It was the ritual of court-ship.

"Do you like to sail?" Peggy asked. Obviously the question was directed at Mark.

"Love it," he responded.

"I have a small sailboat—twenty-six feet. It's down at the marina. Perhaps you'd like to go out to one of the islands sometime."

"Sounds like fun," he said with a smile.

Tracy sighed and toyed with her food. His heart was slipping away, right before her eyes, and there was nothing she could do or say. She was the one who had insisted she didn't love him. It was her fault.

"Peggy seems like a very nice person," Tracy said later, on the drive back to the school and her car.

"She's a gem. Where she gets the energy to cope with a classroom of eleven-year-olds and still do as much as she does, I don't know."

"She's the type of person you admire, isn't she?" Tracy gazed out the side window, a lump forming in her throat.

"Um-hmm," was all he said.

It was evident he wasn't going to voluntarily satisfy her curiosity. She wanted to know if he was going to ask her out, if he liked her enough to do so. More impor-tant, Tracy wanted to know if it was too late, if she'd ruined her own chances with him. But none of those questions came out. Hating herself for being too proud to ask, Tracy rode back to the high school in silence.

The next day she couldn't help wondering if Mark had called Peggy when he got home. Had he set up a sailing date for the weekend? March was a good month for sailing. Springtime. A time when a man's fancy turned to . . . .

She glanced at the clock. Three-thirty. Teachers were supposed to stay on, but today she was going to leave early. Why not? Maybe a stroll along the beach would clear her thinking.

She was walking toward the front doors when Bob came dashing out of Mark's office. "I'm going to be a baby . . . the father's coming," he blurted as he rushed past her on his way to his office.

"Joanne's in labor?" asked Tracy, following Bob into the small room. "Isn't she early?"

"Two weeks. She just called. I was in a meeting with Prescott. Her water broke. Damn, where are my car keys?" he exclaimed, opening and slamming drawers.

"Are these the ones you're looking for?" asked Tracy, holding up a ring of keys that had been dangling over the edge of his picture of Joanne and Amy.

"Oh yeah, I forgot. I put them there so I could find them in a hurry. Thanks, Tracy." He grabbed his jacket from where it lay on the overstuffed chair. "What a day. First Prescott tells me he's recommended me for principal, and now Joanne."

"Principal? How great." Tracy followed Bob out of his office. "Where? For what school?"

"Here—at Dos Pueblos."

"Dos Pueblos?" She stopped abruptly. "But what about Mark?"

"He's leaving. Going to start a private school."

Leaving? Tracy was stunned. She stood in front of the main office, immobilized. It was only as Bob reached the exit doors that she thought to yell, "Good luck. Call me after the baby's born."

Bob was out of sight when Tracy turned to face Mark's office. His door was closed; Mrs. Baines nowhere to be seen. Tracy knew she had to talk to him. He couldn't leave! What would she do without him?

Without thinking, she hurried to his door, and she was turning the knob, even as she knocked. "Mark, Bob said you're...."

Her words died in her throat as she started into the room. Seated in front of Mark's desk were Mrs. Baines, the school superintendent and the head of the school board.

"Tracy?" Mark stood up. "Is something wrong?"

"No, oh dear, I'm sorry. I...I didn't mean to interrupt...I...I'll talk to you later."

Backing out, she closed the door as she left the room. Her face red, she turned to see Rose enter the main office.

"What's up?" her friend asked. "You look like you just caught Mark stark naked."

"I barged in on a meeting of the superintendent, head of the school board and Mark." Her legs felt weak as she walked away.

"Does that mean there's something to the rumor that Mark's leaving?" asked Rose, picking up the notices in her box.

"You've heard it too, then!" Tracy was still slightly dazed.

"Only what Mrs. Baines told Sylvia. Something about some calls. Mrs. Baines was terribly upset. I think she likes our Mr. Prescott."

Mechanically Tracy picked up her own bulletins and shuffled through them. "I think *all* women like Mark."

"So what happened between you two?" Rose asked softly, putting her hand on Tracy's shoulder. "At the Christmas party you both looked so in love. Then, after New Year's, Mark was all scowls and short-tempered and you could have passed for a disaster victim."

"I blew it," Tracy said with a sigh, tears welling in her eyes. "I was so determined not to make a mistake, I made the biggest one of my life. I love him; yet I told him I didn't."

"Why?" Rose shook her head in disbelief. "How could you?"

"I was afraid . . . so afraid I'd be like my mother—and that he'd turn out like Gerry. And now I've lost him." The lump in her throat threatened to silence her. "I can't talk, Rose. I'll see you Monday."

Unable to stop her tears, Tracy hurried out of the school. The drive home was a blur. Like a zombie, she went through the routine of letting in Sam, taking off her dress, pulling on a sweater and jeans, and sorting through her mail. Dinnertime came and went. She opened a can of soup, heated it, poured it into a bowl, then let it sit, untouched.

Tears were finally replaced by a vacant feeling. She turned on the television, picked up a book and stared out the window, not even seeing the gulls swoop and soar. When the sun set, she got up and turned off the TV. Picking up the earthenware pot Mark had bought her, Tracy turned it over in her hands, remembering the weekend they'd spent together, the hours of love they'd shared. How stupid she'd been to turn her back on his love. How foolish. She was sitting in the dark when the doorbell rang.

Snapping on a light, Tracy hurried to the door. "Mark!" she gasped, stepping back in surprise.

"I gathered you wanted to talk to me. This is the first chance I've had to get away. What's the problem?"

"I heard—that is, Bob said—Rose also heard. . ." she stammered, unable to verbalize the dreadful news.

"That I finally found a school." He looked at her, taking in her red-rimmed eyes and her tousled hair, which she'd been anxiously combing her fingers through. "May I come in?"

"Sure." She led the way into the living room. "Do you want anything? Coffee?"

"Maybe later. Sit down, Tracy," he coaxed, seating himself on the nearest couch. "Here, next to me."

She did as he asked, willingly. She was going to lose him. Any time they had together would be time to cherish.

"You knew I was looking for a school," he started. "I told you my plans."

"I know. It's just that. . .well, I didn't think it would be quite this soon."

"The school's on the outskirts of Los Angeles. Perfect for what I need. Dormitories, large classrooms." His face became animated as he described the facilities.

"It sounds wonderful," Tracy said. She wished she could be more enthusiastic, but all she could think of was never seeing him again. "When will you be leaving?"

"Not until June. I have a contract to honor, and several loose ends to tie up before I leave Santa Barbara." He smiled, but she didn't notice.

June. Barely two months and then he would be gone,

out of her life forever. The finality was terrifying. She had to know if there was a chance. "Mark?"

"Tracy?"

They said each other's name together, then self-consciously laughed. "You first," he offered.

"No, after you."

Sitting forward, he faced her. "Tracy, I'm a decisive person—determined, my mother always says. When I was in my teens I saw kids dropping out of school—good talented kids, whom the system had failed. It was then I decided I wanted to reach those students, show them they were as valuable as the honor students and the valedictorians. So I went to college, got a teaching credential, taught, earned a master's in administration and began my training. Now I'm on the brink of realizing my dream."

"I'm happy for you," she said in a low voice, knowing she did feel a pride in his accomplishments.

He hesitated, then took her hand, his eyes delving deep into hers. "The school is important to me, but not half as important as you are. I need to know how you feel about me, if there's a chance for us?"

A chance? Her heart leaped for joy. "But what about Peggy?"

"Peggy?" he asked, his dark brows furrowing. "What about Peggy?"

"I was there last night, remember?" Tracy struggled to keep her emotions under control. "I saw the way you looked at her—the way she looked at you."

"Tracy Dexter," he said, laughing, wrapping his arms around her and gathering her close. "You're acting jealous again."

"I am not!" But a second later she yielded with a tentative smile. "So what if I am?"

"If you are," he growled, giving her a quick kiss on the tip of her nose, "it means you do care, whether you'll admit it or not."

"Oh, I care! Oh, Mark, how I care!" Suddenly she felt optimistic and lighthearted. "And I'll fight off any woman who tries to take you from me. Including Peggy Nichols!"

He was warm and strong, and his chest rumbled with laughter as he hugged her tight. "There's no other woman in my life. There hasn't been since the day you walked into my office, looking more like one of the students than a teacher and daring to defy me when I challenged your integrity. I told you in December I loved you. My feelings haven't changed."

"But all these months—you've been so indifferent, so cold and unemotional!" She couldn't understand.

"Honey, I had to be." Lightly he kissed her lips. "I *am* still your principal."

"But when we were alone in your car? During dinners?"

"Thursday afternoons were my only chance to be with you. Those few hours each week were precious to me. You'd told me you didn't love me, that there was no future for us. Well, I hoped in time you would change your mind. But I couldn't chance saying something too soon and have you refuse to ever go with me again. I didn't dare let you know how much I wanted you."

"Oh, Mark," Tracy groaned, thinking of the past month and how badly she'd wanted his touch. "I was such a fool! I do love you. I love you more than words can express. I realize now you're nothing like Gerry—I'm not even the same person who married Gerry. And I can't go through life afraid to take a chance."

"Will you go with me, then? Marry me? The school deal isn't final. If you don't want to move to L.A., we can stay here until I find another place. It's up to you."

"You'd sacrifice your dream for me?" Tracy stared at him for a moment, then wrapped her arms around his neck and kissed him squarely on the mouth.

"Without you it would be an empty dream," he said deeply when she rested her cheek against his chest.

"Los Angeles sounds just fine. Think there will be a job at your school for a high-school teacher who looks young for her age, acts adolescent at times, and is very jealous?"

"There'll be a job." Mark held her at arm's length. "What about babies, Tracy? Will you have my child?"

"Yes."

"Soon?"

"Yes."

"How about four?" He arched an eyebrow.

"Two?"

"Three?"

"We can argue that later," she replied with a grin.

"No reservations this time? No comparing me to Gerry, or you to your mother?"

"I'm not jumping into this with my eyes closed," she assured him. "These past three months have shown me a great deal about you. I now know that you respect my opinions, that it doesn't bother you when I disagree with you, and that you'll even give in and admit you're wrong. . .occasionally." She smiled. "You planned it this way, didn't you. That's why you picked me as the teacher representative. You knew all along that some-day I'd realize my fears were groundless."

"I prayed you would, but to tell you the truth, your being on the curriculum committee was sheer luck. The superintendent was the one who specifically asked for you. I was so mad at the time that I probably would have picked someone else, then regretted it later. As it worked out, all's well that ends well." He leaned for-ward, his mouth capturing hers.

The telephone rang and Tracy jumped, but she didn't move out of his embrace. By the fourth ring she groaned and went to answer it. She was watching Mark, longing to be back in his arms, when she picked up the receiver.

"It's a boy," Bob announced, half laughing, half cry-ing across the line. "Eight pounds, two ounces."

"Bob has a baby boy, eight pounds, two ounces," Tracy relayed to Mark, then asked Bob, "How's Joanne?"

"Exhausted, but fine. He's beautiful. Matthew Carter Martin. Big hands. A football player if I ever saw one."

"Tell him congratulations," said Mark, rising from the couch and coming to her side. His gaze drifted to the bowl of untouched soup on the dining-room table.

"Mark says congratulations and so do I."

"Mark's there? With you?" Bob asked, his tone in-quisitive.

"He's here," Tracy said, grinning, catching Mark's hand in her own. "We're getting married."

"I don't believe it...I mean, that's wonderful! Oh, I can't wait to tell Joanne. She'll want to know every-thing."

"Tell her that as soon as she feels up to it, we'll come for a visit. I can't wait to see Matthew."

As soon as she hung up the receiver, Mark took her into his arms. "It sounded good to hear you tell Bob we were getting married," he murmured near her ear, his lips nuzzling her neck as his hands slid up under her sweater.

"Hmm," she agreed, as he kissed the sensitive spot at the base of her throat.

"You know, I think you were right. It is your body I want," he groaned, when his exploring fingers discovered she wasn't wearing a bra.

"I don't care." Her nipples hardened and a delightful warmth spread through her limbs. "Oh, Mark, I love you so much."

Raising his head, he smiled suggestively. "Think we could go upstairs for a little while? It's been a long time."

"I'm sure you haven't gone without." She knew for a fact how easily he attracted women.

"There's been no one since you, Tracy."

"No one?"

He shook his head. "It took me a long time to find you. You don't ever need to feel jealous."

Finally she knew it was true. Theirs would be a marriage based on mutual love and trust. Grasping his hand, she led the way up the steps.

"The grunion are running tonight," Mark said, pausing as he loosened his tie. "As I recall, you mentioned you'd like to see that."

"You mean I have to choose between bed and the grunion?" Tracy asked, pulling the bamboo curtain closed.

"No. The paper listed high tide around midnight. We have plenty of time for both." He pulled his unbuttoned shirt from his pants.

"Maybe we will and maybe we won't." Stopping in front of him, Tracy gently twisted several springy dark hairs on his chest between her fingertips. "It's been a long time for me, as well."

Her stomach rumbled and they laughed.

"Whatever you like, but I think we'd better include a hamburger for you in our evening's activities. And speaking of food, how's Sam?"

"Fine. He's missed you."

A smile teased his lips as Mark ran his fingers through her hair and tilted her face up so he could look into her eyes. "More than likely he's missed having a leg to attack. However, I suppose I'd better learn to love your cat, Miss Dexter, because I sure do love you."

"The feeling's mutual, Mr. Prescott." She sighed as his mouth came toward her. "The feeling's mutual."

What romance fans
say about Harlequin…

"Harlequins are the best."
— D.L.* Tampa. Florida

"Excellent…very good reading."
— K.R.P. Burlington. Vermont

"…fresh and original…tremendously
romantic."
— F.V.. Abbotsford. British Columbia

"…Harlequin makes me relax and
dream a little."
— S.L.. Aurora. North Carolina

"…scintillating, heartwarming…
a very important, integral part of mass-
market literature."
—J.G., San Antonio, Texas

"…it is a pleasure to escape behind a
Harlequin and go on a trip to a faraway
country."
—B.J.M., Flint, Michigan

"Their wonderfully depicted settings make
each and every one a joy to read."
—H.B., Jonesboro, Arkansas

*Names available on request.